THE X TRACTOR
Cornwall's Culling Plan

All the very best!

Peter x

THE

TRACTOR

Cornwall's Culling Plan

Peter Spencer

Illustrated by Rory Donald

UNITED WRITERS
Cornwall

UNITED WRITERS PUBLICATIONS LTD
Ailsa, Castle Gate, Penzance, Cornwall.
www.unitedwriters.co.uk

British Library Cataloguing in Publication Data:
A catalogue record for this book is
available from the British Library.

ISBN 9781852001674

Illustrations by Rory Donald
www.reachillustration.com

Printed and bound in Great Britain by
United Writers Publications Ltd.,
Cornwall.

With thanks to all those lovely people whose support, encouragement, local insights and proofreading skills made this book possible. Not to mention all the extraordinary folk whose lives provided inspiration. And, finally, all those decent, hard-working farmers who regularly risk their lives driving tractors on Cornwall's dangerous terrain, and would no sooner deliberately push them over cliffs than eat their own grandmothers.

Contents

Prologue

Good of you to look here. Better still if the good life grabs you. On the Celtic fringe.

Maybe you just want a peek. Or a second home. Maybe even a second chance. A rural idyll, time to be idle.

But the relocation transaction's about more than property. It's where neighbours become good friends. Or not.

To get in there, best acquire relatives in the area. Then you're sorted.

But if you give a flying furrow for the country folk, just for themselves, their story starts here.

Be it Cornwall, Caernarvonshire, Caithness, they're down to earth. All of them. Down in the dumps. Some of them. Down on their luck too, many of them.

Imagine life, real life, in that cosy little cluster of Cornish cottages where you've been so often for those two wonderful weeks in August. Always so welcoming, roses round the doorway. Sheer poetry.

But picture it in prose. Concrete and cream teas. Pasties and pixies. And generally empty holiday homes. In a once proud and crowded place with its own parliament, and masses of tin and must-have minerals vital to the arms race. In the bronze age.

Now that tin's off and bronzing's what you do in the Mediterranean, life ain't easy up West. But it does go on. And how!

There are Proper-Cornishes, with hair growing out of their ears, and money oozing out of their pockets. Strangely, their trousers are held up with binder string, and their nice new Land Rovers look like they've been dropped into slurry pits. Out of aeroplanes.

They plough the fields and scatter the good seed on the ground. And cede none of it to anyone. Better to be hard to get on with than hard up. Not hard to work out.

But they do offer people lifts. Wisely, locals prefer walking. Maybe they study Darwin, round those parts. More likely, it's just down to long and life-threatening experience.

Then, geographically cheek-by-jowl but culturally planets away, there are the Cor-Strewth-Cornishes, who have some (some say too many) ancestors from somewhere more up smoke than up market.

Years ago the missus did the school run in rollers. Now, Rollers are for driving around in instead. With gold bits for door handles. The model of choice? Corniche, stoopid.

And a class act they are too. In a brass-necked way. You always know where to turn if you want to scrap something. And sometimes if you don't. But find it gone anyway. Tractors? Shoved over cliffs? Why do that? Best not ask.

Protest? Pointless. Replacing the teeth it'd cost you would cost more than the goods you'd lost. Since finding an NHS dentist round these parts is harder than getting a tenner out of the tooth fairy.

But getting a few bob out of the insurance industry can be a runner. And that's where the tractors come in. Or, rather, go out. With the tide. That'll be the Fallow-Kernow caper.

Horny handed son of toil that he is, he'll get his hands dirty if needs be. And all the waters of the Atlantic will wash his little hand. And keep alive the devilment peculiar to the duchy. That healthy disregard for order and authority in all its forms. Cornish folklore? Laws are made to be broken. And begger the consequences.

Not that unpleasantness ever unfolds for the Cor-Cor-Cor-Cornishes, by contrast. They go about their strictly lawful business strictly unruffled. Quietly, unassumingly, assuming they're all right for money. Which they are. Old money, naturally. They have perfect manners, and live in manor houses. No need for THEM to steal from anyone. Their family did it for them. Centuries ago.

Stuttering's their st-st-stock-in-trade. And the Stock Exchange their bulwark and refuge.

All so different from the Lord Haw-Haws, who're callow, shallow, and cast a shadow over otherwise popular resorts. Every summer hols. Forget being seen and not heard, they're a herd of half-crazed elephants. Loudly rowdy, and generally a pain in the arsenic and old lace.

Their Mummies and Daddies are rich enough to give them the allowances they so richly don't deserve. Which is how come they're overpaid as well as oversexed. And, to collective local chagrin, over here.

All, doubtless, part of life's rich evolutionary pattern. And ugly ducklings do always turn into graceful swans. Though you never know whether a tadpole will turn into a dear little frog, hopping around daintily, indeed mouth-wateringly if you happen to be French, or a fat, venomous toad.

Odd that they should have gone west at all. As they really are more Bullingdon than Bulmers. Yet they trade, confusingly, as gentle folk.

Though trade, with anything other than mythic gods and goblins, would be out of the question for the The-Cause coven. Paid up pagans all, their homes, wheels, souls, and probably their hamsters and goldfish too are "Protected by Witchcraft". Man.

Dress code, strictly period. Mess code, strictly veggie. Stress code, strictly, ermm, ommmmmmmm. No one who was there remembers The Sixties. Man. These guys don't, because they weren't even born. Most of them. But they're harmless. Look the part and you've joined the club. Joined up thinking? Strictly optional.

Conspiracy theories? Magic! Aliens? Better still. All they need is LOVE, man. For the flowers they put in their hair. While going to San Francisco, in their dreams. And for their Fellow Man, man. Little green chaps from Mars are nirvana. But humans will do.

It's human to err. And to forgive is divine. So, let us pray for the Bible belters. The Reborns. On their piously creaky knees, they're reborn every week, bless'em. Comforting, given how long ago most of them popped out the first time. Not that they remember The Sixties, heaven forfend. At least, not the good bits.

Watch them all spilling, all smiling, out of God's house after their fix of faith, hope and love, the greatest of those being love, and you'd think they'd never stray from the path. At least, never on a Sunday. But coveting thy neighbour's ox is only natural in the country. And why forgive those that trespass against us, when you can tell them to "Get off my bledy land."?

And, oh Lord deliver us from temptation, could there not be more to crucifixion than atonement for original sin and banging up burglars? Maybe a way of nailing thy neighbour. If you don't love him quite enough. Sooner sin than be sinned against? Amen to that!

But the Cornwall-Calling cabal feel seriously sinned against. By marauding hordes lording it over everything, getting in the way, stealing the sunshine, putting up tents and the price of property, eating everything in sight and, very likely, killing the county's first born.

True, a visitor free county would be an even greener land. But pleasanter? With virtually no money coming in? Probably just a lot emptier.

Time was when armed Celts invaded England. And got invaded back, and hacked to pieces. No wonder early Cornishmen linked arms with Viking invaders against Londoners. Which must have really annoyed them. Having your head hewn off by axe wielding maniacs would spoil anyone's day.

Anglo-Cornish tensions subsequently subsided. Along with the fashion for rapine and pillage, once so high in people's list of dislikes. But things are still sent to try us. Like call centres. The Cornwall callers don't actually work in them, but they get the FU UK credo out in the same way.

Think of all those long, useless, expensive calls you've made to someone who keeps saying "no problem" but does nothing whatever with yours, except make it worse. A war of attrition, which you know you're going to lose. Along with the will to live, as the muzak mulches your brains.

These guys operate the same way. You're off to walk the cliffs, wondering how long to the next cove, and the old cove you call out to says it's ten minutes. He means dreckly.

Ten hours, then, at least. Perhaps ten years. You don't know that, but he does. And he knows you don't. Thus has he got you by the baubles.

He seems so quaint, with his ambling ambience and his humbly-bumbly bearing, but beware. And be aware. The Celts saw off the Romans. And the Anglo Saxons. And gave the Normans a hard time too.

Get to know them. Learn to love them. And they MIGHT love you back . . .

1

A Not Quite Everyday Story of Proper Cornish Folk

For Prunella-Proserpina Proper-Cornish the day seemed not to have any surprises in store. Nasty or otherwise. Just the normal Prunella Proserpina Proper-Cornish routine.

Dear, lumpy old hubby had rolled out hours ago, because animals, with no sense of the proper decencies of life, always insist that farmers do things to them at stupidly early hours.

Little wonder that Farmer Proper-Cornish had little time for doing things to his dearly beloved. Decent or otherwise. Either in the morning, when she was snoring on her back under the bedclothes, or in the evening when he'd be snoring on the sofa over the telly.

Sometimes, just sometimes, before falling asleep he would fall to musing. Not very amusingly. On why he was a farmer at all. Maybe, he supposed, for the same reason people live in Dagenham. If it's all you know, that's your world. No matter how horrid.

He'd been to Dagenham once, with his dad. To pick up a tractor engine. Useful. But living there? With no fields or forests and crowds where space is supposed to be. And all that noise, and no comforting good clean country piggy poo smells. Unimaginable. He liked the road out. And that was it.

So farming was his fiefdom. And his destiny. Toil, morning to night. On his tod, mostly. Apart from his four-legged charges. In his way he loved them, but he loved a laugh too. And you can't exactly have that with a flock of sheep.

Different in granfer's day. Hard then. But with more time. And more people. And none of that there Common Market and they there foreign folk telling you you're bad because you're good and how to lie straight in your bed at night. A farmer's lot these days? Nothing but trouble and strife. Of the wrong kind.

Now the right kind of trouble and strife, dear old Prunella-Proserpina, or Pea-Pea as he'd whisper in her ear when doing that there mushy stuff with her, as they did so often in those far gone days before the kids were born, with the result that they WERE born, now she was the best pea in any pod.

Mostly she was easy. Flaccid, but placid. If she blew her stack he'd hide under one. Because he'd probably deserved a good hiding. Under anyone's reckoning. But they jogged along. The affliction of friction had given way to affection years ago. Much easier. Much nicer.

In her youth, Prunella-Proserpina had been a feisty little filly, leading young Proper-Cornish a proper dance before accepting that as she was not, after all, going to be a top model or a film star, she might just as well accept his hand in marriage instead.

And as the years had diminished her dreams they dilated her dimensions. As they do. Having once been coquettishly curvy, she was now positively curvilinear. A sort of blancmange on legs. But still a good sort, under her equivocal visage and flowery apron.

This apron she wore at all times. It was not really a protective garment designed to prevent soil or anything else soiling her pretty pink frocks. Or her grubby boiler suit. Or whatever else she might have flung on that day. It was more a badge of office. A demonstration of domesticity. An ensign enacting her role in the farm. In life. In perpetuity.

In that sense, it WAS a kind of protective garment. Shielding her from those awkward questions that sometimes nagged, prodded, and provoked. Like, what had happened to her dreams? Was she wasting time? Was time now wasting HER? Where was the passion, for heaven's sake? The suspense? Suspenders were the nearest thing she got to that these days. And, face it, that's not even close.

So, instead, she just kept herself busy. Or at least looking it. And her bodily dilation begot spiritual resignation. The wistful glances she stole at her snoring husband had become little more a feature of her life than the mink stole she'd once dreamed he'd give her.

The evenings, then, GENERALLY gave way to dream free sleep. And she began the day in question, as so many others, contentedly brushing sleep from her eyes, along with a couple of stray earwigs and a spider, rolling back bedclothes, and dragging rollers out of hair, indifferent to the Atlantic rollers so importunately pounding away on the beach below.

Odd, that, seeing as there was no wind. But Prunella-Proserpina's only concern was removing random ducks from the washstand. No eggs. No surprise.

Two chickens and a small pig rummaged round in the Aga. A reminder that breakfast beckoned. No problem for chickens, which are merely involved in the process. But bad news for pigs, which are committed.

It looked, though, as if Prunella-Proserpina had some seriously bad news on her plate too. Perhaps it was something in the air. Perhaps the peremptory peal of the telephone. Perhaps both.

Granfer Proper-Cornish had had the instrument installed during The War for advance warning of bombing raids, which so worried the sheep, poor dears. But since then no member of the family had had much time for the nasty, noisy and, unaccountably, smelly thing. Just like Dagenham, Farmer Proper-Cornish always said.

Prunella-Proserpina always agreed. Though she knew not why. Probably because she was shy on the phone. Especially when it rang, as it did today, in that wearisomely Wagnerian sort of way. As though you could wait till the last trumpet and it'd still be ringing. Infuriatingly. Interminably. Loudly.

"Hell-oo-oo," she intoned slowly. "What do you WANT?"

Hardly a gregarious greeting. But Great-Aunt Perdita was as untroubled by nastiness as she was by niceties. Of any kind.

"Hear me, toe of frog," she retorted tartly. Her name, she had discovered in her childhood, was to be found in some dusty old book she'd found propping up a three-legged wardrobe in the attic. It was by one o' they dead people. Some fellow called Shakes-Bake. Or was it Bacon Roll? Or Shakin' Stevens? Anyway, he wrote this really long thing called *Complete Works*.

Disappointed that he'd never written a sequel, Perdita nonetheless consumed its contents (mainly to infuriate her parents), and now prided herself on her command of Elizabethan English. She knew little and cared less what any of it meant. She just enjoyed prattling away at people. Like a small child. Only without the redeeming feature of being sweet.

"Scurvy, infidel, cankerblossomed whore," she continued

in a softer tone. "Wouldst not know what thy doom portends? A sickly end to thy sickly days," she added. Almost caressively. She really did hardly understand anything she said. No matter how hard she listened.

So for Prunella-Proserpina, all this gusty musty stuff from Great-Aunt Perdita was just boringly normal. And yet. And yet . . .

And yet another odd thing happened next.

Cousin Peregrine Proper-Cornish had fled the slurry pit where he'd been doing his farmer's stinky-stuff stuff, leapt into the Land Rover, and swerved, impervious to its imperfect brakes and weirdly veering steering, to Proper-Cornish-Comfort Farm.

The door knocker crashed, smashed, to the ground as he hammered it. No change there then. But his words, when the fine example of late Jacobean but now sadly dilapidated door finally creaked open, were pretty awesome. By his standards. He was slow of speech and seemingly slower still of thought. To get his drift, people generally settled for guesswork.

Poor thing, his card had been marked from infancy by the chance card of fate. The fait accompli of universal ignorance. Twenty years on, people would have heard of the word dyslexia. Probably even managed to teach him to spell it.

And they might have noticed how much more interested the illiterate farm boy was in square roots than root

vegetables. How he could dig out from the back of his mind the square root of any number. And get it right to the nearest recurring decimal point.

But no, teachers just thought he was rambling. And had him down as weird as well as stupid. So, taught nothing, he learned nothing. And, as the years rolled by, he quietly rolled over. And let his brain fur over. The sleeping not the dead, at least. As if you could spot the difference.

Such a waste. He could have turned his mathematical touch into the Midas touch. Become a merchant banker, buying the Guatemalan national grid before breakfast, selling it to South Korea before lunch, and picking up an ocean-going yacht with the small change before suppertime.

But would all that have made him happier? Nicer? An arrogant, rapacious brute? Whatever, just another what-if of history.

And what if Great-Aunt Perdita had been saved for a later generation? Veneration would have been too much to ask. But with a spot of understanding she would have spotted that Asperger's was not a poisonous snake consumed between two halves of a bun. She probably would also have known that Queen Cleopatra's first and last encounter with an asp had ended badly. And could have linked the two ideas in a professional capacity.

Hardly a glittering career, writing cryptic crosswords. But better than just being written off as a lonely old loony.

Such was the injustice they both had to bear. For being

born too soon. Though at least Peregrine was regarded as faintly sane. And was taken faintly seriously when he said, as he now did, quite clearly: "You be 'earin' this, my proper maid, there be queer 'appenin's down they there pits."

It was a start. And, gleaning from his air of swivel-eyed distraction that not all was quite as it should be, Prunella-Proserpina tried a prayer: "Oh god, what's the stupid old duffer on about now?"

But, God being silent on the subject, and Great-Aunt Perdita having apparently taken fright, or another pint of laudanum or whatever, breakfast was going to have to wait. And instead the strangely sulphurous air must be sniffed.

Oh yes. There really WAS something in the air. Even nastier than the standard stench exuding from slurry pits the world over.

And the sheep, Prunella-Proserpina noticed, seemed more than worried. Savagely anxious in fact.

"Be still, my bleating heart," they could have been thinking, as slurry at source oozed from every dear little bilious bottom. And the cattle were on the same mission. Forget good clean country smells. This lot honked.

And bits of sheds and barns, windows and what not, lately hanging, banging and slamming into one another, were bestrewn randomly about the place. Alongside lumps of antiquated rusting farming equipment, with spiky bits sticking out everywhere, that might come in useful some day but somehow never did.

b

More than ever the farm looked a cross between a rubbish dump, a demolition site and a place of medieval execution. Forget 'elf'n'safety, these guys did mortal danger for a pastime.

Strangely, though, in this strangest of all possible days, the abiding sense was that maybe, just maybe, the Worst was already Over.

Even Cousin Peregrine, lately so agitated, now seemed content to gnaw ruminatively on the rum and raisin pasty and slimily mouldy vegetables that had been discolouring his disintegrating pocket.

Prunella-Proserpina looked at him with an infinite weariness, and heaved a sigh. A sigh of sorrow and of yearning. Welling, well earned, but unfulfilled.

Just as the world went weird at the slurry pit, in her unconscious under the eiderdown underworld she too had felt the earth move. And move it had.

But now came the rude awakening – that what had happened had been anything but rude. Not even a bit of fun. Just another beastly reminder that no married woman is ever attractive, except to her husband. And sometimes not even to him.

So much for the Real Thing, it was obvious what this was. Just another bloody earthquake.

And yet, it was unsettling. The roof could have caved in on her. Forget the peace that's past all understanding, she could have been past tense. And the fact that any day could be your last is an argument against sleepwalking through life. The same as a machine-gun pointed at your head.

So something stirred. With the passage of time blurred. But stirred nonetheless. And the sturdy little filly in her flickered fitfully back to life. The cat noticed. The dog noticed. Even the budgerigar seemed to take the hint.

As for Farmer Proper-Cornish, plodding wearily home that night, epiphany awaited. The telly so bedecked with flowers the screen was nowhere to be seen. Likewise the flowery apron. Instead, Prunella exuded expensive French fragrance. Of gardenias. His favourite, as they both knew. From so long ago.

Oh yes, the maid had made an effort. But not made herself ridiculous. The subtle but unmistakable touches to dress, coiffure, makeup. "Pardon me, Pea Pea," he murmured meaningfully: "The gentleman must please adjust his dress."

No doubt about it, the gentleman's suit is more figure-flattering than the boiler suit. And putting a comb through the hair is hardly a mortal sin. Likewise, hanging up one's boots. At least for the evening. Which was languorously lubricated, as it turned out, with the litre of sherry that had been hanging around since Christmas.

In vino veritas? In this case, veritably. As the home truths poured out, along with the sherry, in ever greater measures. About who they might have been. And who they were well on the way to becoming. Not through any conduct unbecoming, mind. Just through getting into the kind of rut that made what was left of the lane, mentioned in the Doomsday Book and little maintained since, look like some silkily soignée German autobahn.

And they started as they determined to keep on. A quick blast on the nasty, noisy but for some reason not quite so smelly telephone, and cousin Peregrine was up for getting up. For the early turn. Even for getting a bit of help around the place.

"With what we turned over last year," he drowsily drawled, "we could manage four extra hands, expanding production by twenty-two point three two five nine eight four percent. Less twelve point nine nine nine nine six in they there wages and insurance, that be a net gain of nine point three two six zero two four points. Should pay for seventy-six point zero zero zero seven of one of they self propelled forage harvesters within forty-nine days, eighteen hours and four seconds."

Cousin Peregrine's longest speech since childhood. Farmer Proper-Cornish's sharply and audibly indrawn breath was among his shortest. But life on the land did become easier. Not overnight, and hardly cakes and ale, but fun. Surprisingly often.

And Peregrine's money-making schemes became surprisingly creative. He even fantasised about chucking that there tatty old tractor over a cliff, to pick up the insurance, as he'd heard others were wont to do. But in the end he found the idea wanting. On the grounds that it was too Jamaica Inn.

Of course, there was room at the inn for Great-Aunt Perdita on high days and holidays. She was a prescribed presence at such times. But nowadays she seemed softened. Still incorrigibly incomprehensible. But taking her texts these days more from the comedies than the tragedies.

As for Prunella-Proserpina and her other half, it felt like the better half of life was just beginning. The lights were on again. All night sometimes. And upstairs too.

In his youth, Farmer Proper-Cornish had been an amateur pilot. A quick refresher course and he got his wings back, and his wife aloft. So much for cold comfort, this was sizzling . . .

2

Cor-Strewth-Cornish
Capers Capped

Gaffer Godfrey stared menacingly out of the tiny window of his tiny cottage, pressed his knuckle into his close-cropped temple, and declared gruffly: "I'll be avenged on the whole pack o' ye." He didn't mean any such thing, of course. But a good grumble was a soothing sedative. As it so often is.

He contemplated his decayed but still flint-hard frame, fiercely tightened the filthy old rugby club tie he used as a belt, hunted out his cracked and crinkled old boots, and was cheered to find each contained a bottle of stout. Full, fortunately. And the sun was over the yardarm. Double result.

Life had been good to him. For a good long time. Amazingly so, considering his lifestyle. Till the great axe fell. Gertie. "How bledy dare she?" He demanded of no one

in particular. "She'm got no right to bledy leave me all on me bledy tod." No one's perfect, he conceded to himself, but being dead really was a bit much.

Besides, he freely acknowledged, verbally shaking one's fist at the world, or just generally setting it to rights, works better with an audience in tow. Merely saying it to oneself makes one feel, well, a bit of a nutter.

God, how he missed the old bird. They'd jogged along together for so long. Losing her, just like that, when women are supposed to last longer than men anyway, made him feel like his legs had been sawn off. Above the knee, needless to say.

After all these years playing the indomitable force, as well as the local scallywag, willing to take on anybody or anything, this was his darkest hour. His already ebbing strength was sorely sapped. Supping on liquids helped. And increasingly he was discovering that he could overcome everything except temptation.

And here was his difficulty. Like an ugly seaside town that looks momentarily silky as the setting sun softens its lines, his days took on a cheer with those first few pints. That all too often dissolved into disillusion as the nights wore on. Then his hurt could translate to anger, directed at those he valued most.

Topping that list was that top geezer from up the smoke whom he'd so nurtured, nature's gent if ever there was one, the bruiser at the boozer on a bad night, but mostly a gem. Uncut of course. But still the business.

That George Cor-Strewth-Cornish. In god's truth, the old Gaffer admitted to himself, he could take anyone for a ride. Including him at times. But you had to make allowances for anyone who'd been on a journey like his. From the Balls Ponds Road, via Pratt's Bottom, to the Cornish arcadia of his dreams. A steep and stony path. And a bit roundabout. More circles of hell than South Circular.

It took years. And years off George's life, all that learning to not be who he thought he was. And discovering that here in Cornwall everybody knew exactly who you were even if YOU didn't.

In the big city, a wide boy could give people a wide berth when he'd done the dirty on them. In the depths of the countryside you couldn't exactly melt into the crowd. Humans tend to be a bit conspicuous among a herd of cows. They can low to their hearts' content, but lying low at a different local is tricky when there's only the one.

George had been brought up to believe that in all important matters it is style, not sincerity, that is the essential. But for some annoying reason, he slowly and painfully found out cutting a dash didn't cut it in quite the same way round these parts.

Poor thing. In earlier times he rejoiced in the nickname "Gorgeous" George. Here, when he turned fifty he had to stop being fashionably thirty-nine, or even thirty-nine and some months.

And, as the joke wore thin, his person travelled in the

opposite direction. The six-pack to die for now a creaky old barrel of warm flat beer. The ponytail too, once the jewel in his crowning glory, grew meagre. Still blond. Still there. But only just. More Poirot than Bardot.

Still, a glug of Nescaif and a few gaspers would get him on the frog and toad again. Bluster? He could muster that.

"You wanna geddit done? We'll sortit. Right? You don't wanna geddit done? We'll still sortit. And it'll costya more. Geddit?"

Oddly enough, in the neighbourhood, not everyone was a member of his fan base. "Base sort of fellow," more often the verdict.

But the cannier Cornish clocked that in time he'd connect with his inner cuddly toy. Not exactly sweet and pink and fluffy, and definitely in need of a trip to the dry cleaners. But still a world away from his Richardson relatives from Sarf-Lunnon. Beloved of their mums they may be, and not given to hurting flies. But there was a problem with people. And nailing heads to coffee tables is not, on balance, a very nice thing to do.

Sure, up the smoke, George had had enemies. And he brought one with him. Himself. Aping, as he could, the little monkey he'd been in his youth. Stupid. He'd escaped to the country to get away from the roughnecks who could so easily have broken his.

"If you don't want the time, don't do the crime," his silk said after that last job that went so wrong and so nearly put him on a ten-year diet of porridge. Which he didn't even like as a kid.

As a kid, though, he once had a holiday in Cornwall. Dad was banged up, as usual, but Mum had a lucky flutter on the gee-gees. And that was when the beautiful friendship with Gaffer Godfrey began. Not that friendship between rough and ready fellows like these two is always exactly alluring of aspect. A bit too willing to be rough, sometimes, even with one another. But always ready to make up. Eventually.

First off, however, it was his mum to whom the Gaffer took a fancy.

But he planted a seed in the boy's mind. If not, in the event, in his mother. It was a lifestyle thing. Ducking and weaving, the same as him and his mates, but sorting sties and doing deals that didn't have the other sort of pigs on his back. Result.

No doubt about it, the Gaffer was the business. Wiry, wily and wilful, and a character. Albeit a bit flawed. Feared and revered by local lads, with a reputation in which he revelled. And a marriage in which he rejoiced. In spite of the odd foray down the primrose path of dalliance.

Not that he ever got anywhere. Luckily for him. In a village everyone knows your business. Especially if it's monkey business. Nudge, nudge. Say no more.

And what could he say when Mrs Cor-Strewth gave him the peroxide brush-off and medusa stare. And told him to zip it, sling his hook, keep it in his trousers and one or two other choice things of her choice, with a few good old Anglo-Saxon adjectives thrown in? Not much.

Though when it came to it, or, rather, didn't, he was surprisingly gracious. "No offence, lady. We country lads am not used to your type round these parts. Proper turns our heads, see. But you'm still proper. And your boy. He'm well proper too."

Indeed, long after the allure of the brass visaged bimbo with the crimped ringlets and astonishing cheekbones had passed into oblivion, the gobby little upstart she had in tow tugged at his memory. He vowed that if ever the lad took flight to Cornwall he'd see him right.

Which was lucky for George Cor-Strewth. As he needed all the help he could get when he did finally touch down in the village. Seeing as he equated rustics with ruminative quadrupeds, and told them so. To their faces. To their chagrin. Hardly surprisingly.

The move certainly was a right kick up the Khyber. For a start, everyone seemed to know the missus. All instinctively called her Moll. And equally instinctively recoiled from his bare chest and bling, clapped out customised Corniche Roller, and dodgy Cockney accent.

How was he to know they didn't trust anyone from another hamlet, let alone another planet? In his case, in their view, planet clink.

Of course, the old trick of prising open a closed

community by acquiring relatives in the area was not a runner for George. One parent, of either gender, would have been quite sufficient. But there's no getting round it, Belmarsh is a long way from Bodmin. Same as Benidorm. Which was why Mum couldn't be any help either. Now that she was set up and living the life of riley with one of Dad's more fortunate former business associates.

Thus it fell to Gaffer Godfrey, in loco parentis, to keep his promise to himself and his protégé out of trouble. As best he could. Not easy with someone like George. The more unsure he was of himself, the more mouth and trousers he was with everyone else. The blagger with the swagger. He just couldn't help it. Everyone's got to be someone.

"Bleedin' stoopid farmers," he'd tell the world and his wife down the pub: "Why'd they go slogging their bleedin' guts out day in day out fer bleedin' ha'pennies? When all they gotta do is chuck their rusty old tractors over the cliff and get new ones off the insurance. Tea leaf, moi? Bleedin' obvious, innit? I'll bleedin' do it for them. And go halves on the payout. If they're lucky. Sorted."

"But it ain't no bledy good you acting like you'm the only one with any bledy brains," the Gaffer testily pointed out. "They'm goin' know you'm takin' the bledy piddle when you diddle them."

All arguments are vulgar. And all too often convincing. More's the pity, thought George, seeing as he had already taken a solemn vow to give up his more colourful commercial practices now that he was trying to settle in a rural setting. Giving up colourful language, however, was going to have to wait.

He'd been charmed by the story of a harassed and oil-smeared young private on national service crawling out from under a broken-down truck and responding to an officer's query, as to the nature of the problem, in the following terms: "The ****ing ****er's ****ing ****ed. Sir."

It was the clean linguistic lines that so appealed. As well as the Anglo-Saxon simplicity. And what worked for the soldier back then worked for George now: "You ****faced old ****er," he told the Gaffer. "It's got ****all to do with you what I ****ing do to put ****ing bread on the ****ing table. So just **** off, and take a flying **** at the ****ing moon." Clear, vivid, and relatively concise. But a less than generous way of dealing with what was, after all, meant as helpful advice.

Under normal circumstances, the only thing to do with advice, helpful or otherwise, is to pass it on. But on this occasion, George knew, he was going to have to take it. Especially as it was his own idea in the first place. Inwardly, he was resolved to shake the old man's hand and call him brother. But not before he'd called him a great many other names first. Bad form otherwise.

There was also the question of how to go about going straight. Breaking the habit of a lifetime takes time. And experimentation. And determination. But he was nothing if not a trier. And was amazed to find if you can organise a protection racket you can sell a tennis racket. Straight. And at a profit.

His first breakthrough. When the sports hall burnt down, contents lost, he revived a lost connection and got a job lot. Nice one. He told the council he'd throw in the lorry the stuff fell off and all. They only half bought the story, but took all the gear.

And the blaze warmed the cockles of his heart. He'd always fancied being an arsonist, but now realised you don't have to start fires to see them. And putting them out's just as much fun. So he joined the local volunteer brigade. Locals liked him for that. In spite of themselves.

"Just casing the joint," he'd joke while clambering over smouldering roofs. Given their own recreational pursuits, some of the younger ones wondered if the gangster was also an international drug runner. Easy mistake to make.

And mistakes in translation were par for the course in George's early good-life days. Like the day in the butcher's when he told the geezer behind the counter: "Stop rabbiting on the dog and bone, get on yer plates of meat and show me what ya got. I wanna good butcher's."

The good gentleman was about to suggest he beggar off out his bledy shop when he was interrupted by a second customer. One o' they old farmers from up the moors. A rare old beauty. Boots bodged up with rusty nails and even his hat held together with binder string. Unusual, even by moorland standards.

Seeing as the old recluse exclusively lived on road kill, there was no telling what he was doing in the butcher's. Or what he was saying. Which was a pity. As it might have been really interesting.

But the butcher, himself a broad Cornish speaker, was no more savvy than the Cockney. Though, as chair of the local historical society, he wondered whether the native language really did die out in 1676. Was it still alive and kicking? Surely not. Not in THOSE boots.

Anyway, from this sea of confusion, he could see the point of the Pals' Brigades in 1914. Recruited from the same communities so they could at least understand one another. Confronted by the shower in this shop, the Kaiser would have walked it.

But George was no walkover. Not that day. Not ever. Crossed, he got so cross he'd even scare himself. Luckily, the dogs always helped calm him. Doberman Pinschers? Stoopid, soppy, pussycats more like. Called, respectively, Ruff and Diamond.

And diamonds they were too, the day Gaffer's grandson goofed.

No one in the village knew that on the edge of the moor, near ex-Gorgeous George's gaff, there lurked a long forgotten shaft from a long abandoned mine, obscured under a bush and an absolute death trap.

Picture the lad, then. One minute happily hunting a lost football, the next nearly lost to this world. No one in sight. And no one to hear his cries as he frantically clutched thorny branches. Legs flailing. Strength failing.

The dogs' good sense and keen senses were all that stood between a happy ending and slow, agonising torture. Parents panic-stricken when the boy didn't come home. Interminable, fruitless searches. Darkening suspicions that he'd been abducted. Maybe murdered. A family blighted. And, with no body, no closure.

No such thing happened, though, as Ruff yelped like a dog possessed by the stricken child, Diamond bounded like another dog possessed to the village, and the combined canine emotion and commotion alerted the community.

So the kid didn't cop it after all. His mother was traumatised. His father a soggy heap of sobbing gratitude. And George was suddenly seriously gorgeous. The locals' non-local local hero. Just for having bought the dogs in the first place.

He loved it. Well, who wouldn't? But he was humbled. It wasn't him that'd done good. And he'd done bad in his time too. Thanks to that temper of his. "I'll have the peelings on you, losing your intemperate me," Moll once threatened. She could be so deliciously Moll Malaprop. It was one up on rhyming slang. And it always worked.

"Aw, put a clock in it. I'll have your sluts for barters," George bellowed back. Before they both fell about laughing.

Not half as hysterically, though, as Cor-Strewth and Gaffer that night in the pub, as the full enormity of the so narrowly averted tragedy descended.

Bit of a bloke thing, that, getting sloshed, instead of getting stuff off your chest. Stuff you'd been meaning to say for years. Like, in George's case, "I wish I'd had you for me old dad, me old china." And, in Gaffer's case, "Only ever made maids. Should've had a boy. Like you."

But no, their way of bonding was bandying badinage. About Cor-Strewth's roots. And Pratt's Bottom. Nice little village, Sarf-East London. And not the only place on the planet, it pleased him to point out, with a really stoopid name.

Understandable, the chap being a bit defensive about bits of his background. It happens. Ask anybody from Sarfend.

"I'll 'ave you know there's somewhere in Cornwall called Cocks," George loftily proclaimed, "and a dive in Dorset called Shitterton." He omitted reference to a road called Back Passage. Too close to his old stomping ground. And he wasn't that Brahms and Liszt.

But harmony, of a sort, was soon restored. As old Gaffer slumped at the old Joanna, and gave it a bit of *My Old Man*. "Follow the van, and don't dilly Dante on the way," crooned Cor-Strewth.

He was as mad as Moll about Malapropisms. Without even noticing. But it was his life's journey, the circles of hell, repeating on him. Like undercooked onions.

Anyway, they did it all again at Christmas. George and Moll, Gaffer and Gertie. A real family do. Doing their homework in advance for the festive fun. A competition, for who could name the silliest street, the most vilified village, the rudest rural district.

Twatt in Shetland was a hit. Though Gertie got a bonus for pointing out there was somewhere in Orkney also called Twatt. George scored with Fanny Hands Lane in Lincolnshire, but Moll put him in his place with Spanker Lane in Derbyshire.

And when he tried to top it with Beaver Close in Surrey she holed in one with Butt Hole Road. In Yorkshire. As it happens.

Under the mistletoe, underneath the arches, bit under the weather on Boxing Day, but still instilled with a deep sense of mutual belonging. For ever and ever. As they thought.

But thought's the slave of life, and life's time's fool. And time, that takes survey of all the world, must have a stop. Alas. Poor Gertie.

Even when the missus headed for the hayricks in the sky, though, Gaffer took his loss without losing his balance. At first. But slowly, inexorably, he took a tumble. Tumbler followed tumbler faster and faster.

Then the shorts, in short order. Till he wasn't there for anyone. Not for George and Moll. Not for himself. Not even for the cat for god's sake.

Of course, he'd already shrunk. His strength ebbing as the

years flowed, the one-time lord of George's manor now more the aged retainer. Like posh people's nannies. Surplus to requirements, but still adored by grown up ex charges.

In this case the ex charge charged a delightfully low rent for the delightfully low ceilinged cottage he'd kitted out for the dear old chap. George was determined to dote on him, in his dotage. Or at least do the same for the Gaffer as he'd done for him. See him right.

All he could see now, though, was a shambling wreck. Brutish, broke, and indifferent to the mounting mountain of empties littering his lawn. Where Gaffer Godfrey ended and the rest of the world began, a bad space.

Lost kinships, inevitable. But to George Cor-Strewth, insufferable. The surrogate dad going the same way as the real one. Who hadn't been up to much in the first place. All so not what the stork under the gooseberry bush had in mind.

All it took was a small matter over small change, as far as George was concerned, and sullen words turned into sudden fury. The pent up upsurge of savagery, of pain suppressed since childhood.

Luckily, on the day of the big barney, both men were pie-eyed. No black eyes, then. Only black looks, dark thoughts, and totally useless attempts at putting one another's lights out.

A gaggle gathered and sniggered as the two bruisers hurled insults and whatever projectiles came to hand at one another. Empty beer cans, clods of earth, sticks and stones. Even empty fag packets. Not exactly the nuclear option.

At borstal they'd made George do the church thing, and he hazily recalled the words: "Let he who is without sin cast the first stone." Or something like that. He was stoned at the time.

What HAD he thrown at Gaffer last night? Strewth, not stones? He could only hope none of them had hit him. Or anyone else, for that matter.

Waking without a hangover usually means you aren't going to feel any better all day. So that day Cor-Strewth and the gaffer did. A lot.

It was a bit of a setback, then, for the old man, when he spied his ex gorgeous ex protégé tottering towards him bearing a big black bag. A chainsaw? A shotgun? A gallon of battery acid? Just when he was hoping to make his peace with the guy too.

But what happened next made him cry. Not very blokeish. But real tears. Of real happiness. As George Cor-Strewth murmured softly: "Forget the debt, mah son. And the rent. The cottage is yours. For life. For free."

It wasn't the money, though that helped of course, it was the babe in the wood. The lad loved as his own. Till it all got sluiced away in bereavement's bitterness.

"YOU call ME my son," he sobbed, "my son. . . my son. . ."

"Button yer lip," cut in Cor-Strewth, "it's quivering, mah son." There. He'd said it again. Got the old man in a right two and eight. Still, he cheered up lots when he saw what was in the bag.

Enough lethal fluid, certainly, to kill a horse. But only if taken at one gulp. Which would have been a terrible waste of perfectly good vodka, tomato juice and Tabasco sauce.

Bless them both, before long their hearts were like two singing birds. Though it'd take a queer bird to sing, as they did, to the tune of *Tipperary*, "Take a long shot . . . of bloody Mary".

Next stop, the pub. Its name nodded to the area's mining past. And its punters got oliver twist to the words warbled, to the tune of *Pack up your Troubles*, "Stack up the doubles . . . in Ye Olde Pit Nag."

A right shindig. Cor-Strewth coughed up for it all. And they loved him for that and all.

But eventually poor old Gaffer picked up the tab too. As the tidal wave of snout and booze finally knocked the nelly out of him. He'd seen out his span, though. Or most of it. More than he deserved, doctors would say. Though George would say they're full of tom tit.

Deeds, however, matter more than words. And at the end he was there. At the bedside. To hear the old rascal's final rasp. "It's up the apples and pairs for me. My son."

3

Killing Kafka

Keef Kafka looked despairingly at Kevinia. Wife of fifteen fine years, mother of two lovely children. His, as well as hers, sweet old-fashioned things that they were. He'd promised her the good life, and no one objects to a quiet life. But the silence could be eerie. Silence of the lambs? No mint sauce here. It was a bit TOO quiet on the western front.

It was all so different when they'd come to Cornwall on holiday. People seemed so kind. So open. So obligingly happy to open their doors to help them kindly spend their money. Little did they know how obliged these folk were when they and their ilk took themselves and their shiny cars back to their shiny homes. Somewhere else. The other side of the Tamar. The right side, from the locals' perspective.

It's always hard enough muscling in on any manor where you're a stranger. But, poor Keef, poor Kevinia, nothing was ever quite as it seemed. Was this a Kafka thing, Keef

48

wondered, this never exactly getting a handle on things? After all, the estate where they'd bought their comfortable little modern house looked similar to the one they'd left behind. Just, well, quieter.

But when dear little Abigail turned thirteen, soon after they'd moved in, the moment seemed to have arrived. The moment for breaking the ice. Not Scott of the Antarctic, mind. No "I could be gone some time." Just drop in some time, like, now, please, for Abigail's party.

This was the first misshapen initiation into the shape of things to come. Unlike Hitler in the 1936 Berlin Olympics, they were not able to report that they all came. In fact, hardly anyone did. And Kevinia had gone to all that trouble, too. Baking all those pasties just so all the locals could feel at home. Which, in point of fact, they were. Unlike Keef and Kevinia. Who were going to have to wait a lot longer. And learn a lot more.

Not that they expected things to be exactly as they were when they were bucket and spade trade. But Keef did think he'd struck gold when the manager offered him the transfer from the home counties to the west country patch. His chance to enjoy the job AND the view. Make his dream come true. And give Kevinia and the kids the better life he'd always promised.

After all, selling insurance, while perhaps not quite as glamorous a pursuit as, say, being the first astronaut to walk on the moon, or the most lusted after matinee idol on the

c

planet, is still steady and dependable. And the same more or less anywhere.

Or, at least, so Keef supposed. Little grasping the Cornish perspective on a calling of this nature. In a penal colony the executioner tends not to be the most popular kid on the block. Likewise the insurance salesman in a country colony. Especially one like Cornwall. There are sensitivities, see, about certain commercial practices less common elsewhere.

Mr Kafka contemplated his stock of worthy worldly goods. The bookcase in the living room with the rows of leather bound volumes. Never opened, of course. Condensed classics and encyclopedias are not intended to be actually read, silly. Any more than the hundreds of top tunes from the classics are intended to be listened to. Being seen and heard is what the telly's for, surely.

"Kevinia, dear lady wife, I love you madly. You're all I've got. Well, apart from the car, the house and the kids, obviously," Keef remarked plaintively.

"Well, Keef. I AM all you've got. Apart from the car, the house and the kids, obviously," replied his dear lady wife. "Although we share and share alike. So what's yours is ours and what's mine's me own," she added playfully.

But the undertone was not undetected. Even in the bosom of his loving family, Keef was lonely. And so was Kevinia. Up the road, down the road, inroads of a social nature were not happening. The lights were obstinately stuck on red. Not even flashing amber. Just, wretchedly, red.

51

Old farmer Fallow-Kernow next door was typical. Twinkly eyed, ruddy faced, rustic voice and seemingly every item of apparel held together with binder string. Was that really necessary? Or was he a bit of a fashion victim? In a farmery sort of way. Probably he was.

But more to the point, when he'd made the impossibly unhomely Home Farm and the impossibly draughty barns into holiday lets and moved into the estate he brought a way of thinking with him. As well as five chickens, two pigs, an amazingly unkempt sheepdog and a feral cat.

Not that he was in the Proper-Cornish league, mind. Just a smallholder with an eye for the main chance. And as healthy a regard for the traditions of his calling as disregard for the norms of anyone else's.

What's more, he could afford neither the inhibition of the Proper-Cornishes, nor an intermediary like Cor-Strewth to execute his culling plan. To raise the readies needed to complete the conversions to secure his future.

Of course, he'd still keep his hand in down the farm. So he'd still need a tractor. Or, at least, one tractor. But not the five rotting old hulks that lurked about the place somewhere, and coughed and spluttered into life somehow. Sometimes.

"I'll get they beggers off my bledy land if it's the last bledy thing I do," he ruminated cheerfully to himself. "And they'll pay for the privilege. Handsomely, my handsome."

The holiday lets were a no-brainer, seeing as old Fallow's farm was right on the cliff top. And the discreet disposal of the tractors whose demise would make the project a runner was equally cut and dried, or, rather, cut and drenched, for the same reason.

So simple. All you did was point the old mechanical dray horse at the drink, don't cut the engine but run like hell, and ... see how she flies!

And old Fallow was nobody's fool. If the tractors were to shuffle off down the route marked 'new for old', he was going to take a trip up the long and windy road himself. A few times, in fact. As he'd clocked that insurance companies prefer to accumulate money than spend it. Unlike Oxfam or Help the Aged. Annoyingly.

"Don't seem right to me, they not wanting to part wi' they there pennies," he told his ever attentive if frequently gratuitously savage cat, Fang. "Not that I've ever had much luck wi' either they there accumulation or they there spendin' up till now.

"But the times they be achangin'. You mark my bledy words my bledy handsome. There'll be fresh fish for you on they there Fridays. You won't be havin' to hunt your own bledy food no bledy more," he concluded, confidentially. Fang yawned. Conspiratorially.

Farrow's forays into crime were blissfully straight-forward. If a shade repetitive. Off to the swimming pool then the barber's for a wash and brush up, in that order. Next to the wedding hire shop for binder-string-free togs, then off in the train, incognito.

And in some anonymous little office in some faceless little town he'd take out the policy. One tractor at a time. One company per tractor. Each one was fooled. The plan was foolproof. Only the tiniest economy with the actuality and the Fallow fortunes flourished.

Nothing could go wrong. Nothing at all. No ifs. No buts. No exceptions.

But there was an 'unfortunately'. A minor unanticipated and unsought setback. In the unremarkable, and at the time unremarked shape of Keef Kafka. With his middlingly greying hair framing his middlingly forgettable features, his mid-grey suit, white shirt and really rather incongruous blue tie, he was the fogey that fashion forgot. Far from showing the influence of too many schools, this was the ensemble of aesthetic imbecility.

Shame, as he was rather a decent chap. A dedicated scout leader and accomplished scuba diver. Rather more scope here in Buckinghamshire for the former than the latter, but he prayed for change. For the chance too for his dear lady wife to vent more readily her passion for maritime ornithology. And that the kids might live out their natural kiddie span, instead of being turned perforce into tweenies at the age of five, teenagers at ten, and precocious little turds for ever amen.

And all that would come. Or happily, in the case of the dear little darlings, not come. For now though, Keef was Mr Normal of Nowhere, settling for two weeks a year in the place of his dreams, and the unwitting partner in crime, just this once, with Farmer Fallow.

Not that he recognised this Fallow fellow when he moved in next door to him twelve months later. He wouldn't, would he? The spruced up spiv in the flamboyant flute was a world away from that there farmer with the binder string, and bristling chin and manner to match, with him at least, down here in Cornwall.

Keef, by contrast, was every bit as recognisable, and incongruous in Cornwall as John Major had once been on a Prime Ministerial visit to Asia. A little splash of grey in an otherwise colourful continent. Almost incontinently inappropriate.

So, inevitably, Farmer Fallow was on a mission to omit this missionary from middle England from the Cornish calendar of social events. Great, small and all points in between. Call it ostracism. Call it excommunication. The old ex-tractor trick must remain excluded from public perusal. Or at least from the prying eyes of the unCornish uninitiated.

And what a head start Fallow had on his poor unsuspecting mortal foe. A bit like for the Americans in the South Pacific, it was one Pearl Harbor moment after another. Boom! No invite to the get slaughtered at the harvest festival wine tasting. Crash! No invite to the kids' crèche creative origami course. Wallop! Not even an invite to the bring your own battery Ann Summers saucy surprise party.

It was just too bad. But Farrow, Fats to his mates on account of his musical activities on the local pub gig scene, was in with everyone. And Keef and Kevinia were out. As a consequence, they hardly got out. At all.

Such a shame. They'd have loved Fats Farrow and the Rhythm and Boozers down the boozer. But social climbing wasn't in it. More north face of the Eiger than Blueberry Hill. Even Abigail, and her dear little sister Annabel, sensed the icy blasts and wondered what they'd done.

"I mean, like, it's like we're like, well, like, not, like, liked," complained Abigail, who had so mastered the patois obligatory to all teenagers that she simply could not fathom why she should, like, be, like, not liked like.

Dear little Annabel, as yet five years shy of turning teen, sometimes struggled to grasp her sister's meaning in all its meandering linguistic detail. But she got the underlying drift, and shared the uneasy sentiment.

As the fickle finger of fate would have it, however, dear little Annabel also shared with Farmer Fallow a fondness for the birds. Of the feathered variety. To that extent they were birds of a feather, so to speak. Thus flying in the face of their Montague versus Capulet capacity for enmity.

"Oh Romeo, Romeo, wherefore art thou Romeo?" dear little Annabel demanded. Or would have done, had she realised what crinkly old Fallow next door was really up to, as she stood on her balcony proffering food for the daily more trusting sparrows, thrushes, robins and house martins.

In truth, he was in a state of mortal combat with himself, as he watched the dear little girl help minister to the flock he'd so nurtured for so long. Most people, he mused, seemed hardly to notice the fragile little creatures that bring such music into our lives. And kids are the worst.

"But this one, why she be almost bledy human. Proper, she is. An' they birds, they get hellish hungry come bledy winter. If decent souls don't feed them they bleedin' headed for that there nasty nest where they bledy go but don't come back."

Strange how some farmers can make their living out of taking lives, but be as soppy as you like with other animals when survival's not at stake. It shows that killing's not necessarily personal. Like the Christmas truce in 1914. Whizzo chums one minute. Whizz-bangs and machine guns the next. Bonkers, or what?

But in the end, Fats Fallow's soft underbelly got the better of him. He was vulnerable to attack round there, as one is, and the little girl's unspoken appeal to his better nature utterly demolished his defence.

"Look, maid," he confided in dear little Annabel. "You'm proper, see. I ain't got nothing against you. Nor your dad, really. It's just his bledy job, see. Round these parts we'm not fond o' they there bledy vermin, see. We got our ways, see. And it be best they don't see. See?"

It was quite a pleasant change for Farmer Fallow, for so long a widower and for so long therefore forced to settle for

Fang as a confidant, to be able to share his thoughts with an actual person. Albeit rather a small one.

But pity poor dear little Annabel. What with her big sister talking teen and this old bloke just being apocryphal, what with all those weird words and weird way of saying them, she was beginning to wonder if it were her or the others in need of a visit to the funny farm.

Next, however, the old man said something she did understand. About how he could get her dad a nice job as a postman. That way, he'd always be home in the evening to read her a story. And, probably, when he finished his rounds, the postmaster would give him sweets for her as well.

Dear little Annabel. In her dear little forgetful ten-year-old developmental stage she couldn't remember how she'd talked the old man round to her point of view. In fact, she couldn't remember using any words at all. But he clearly was seeing things her way. Ergo, she must have convinced him. As grown ups never, ever, begin by seeing anything from a sensible point of view.

Anyway, all she had to do now was convince Daddy that it was time he called time on that boring job he'd brought with him from Buckinghamshire, that had him driving around for days at a time and was clearly driving him mad, as he always seemed to look worried and miserable when he did get home.

Little did she know that persuading Daddy to do just that was going to be about as difficult as persuading a seventeen year old boy to drive suicidally fast in the sports car of his choice, or a young woman of similar years to commit financial suicide with a Harvey Nicholls credit card.

For the truth was that poor Keef Kafka was getting it in the neck every which way. Most farmers to whom he tried to sell insurance were so given to telling him to get off their bledy land that he'd begun to wonder if he could give the stuff away. And that which he did manage to sell had the horrid habit of biting back. What was it about tractors round these parts, he wondered, that made them so prone to falling off cliffs?

The boss wondered that too. And wondered what the game was. And whether Keef was in on it. Which he wasn't. All he wanted was to earn enough money to be able to stay where he was, put on his sub aqua gear and gawp at a few fishes. And maybe help out in the scout hut if they'd have him.

And he was being had all right. Farmer Fallow had seen to that. But now that Keef was up for seeing things his way he was going to see him right, see? It was all so stupidly easy. Made falling off a log seem like persuading Niagara Falls to flow the other way.

So, death to the harassed and hard pressed insurance salesman. And life to the happy-go-lucky postie. Keef slung the grey suits, the Valhalla collection as he'd have been minded to call them if he'd heard of the word, and chuckled at the recollection of even the charity shop saying they didn't want them. So much for making ugly things for the poor. Let the devil wear Prada. They'll settle for their pride.

And, along with the dress code, Keef cut the dreary hairstyle too. OUT went the slightly sheepish sheared look, and IN came exuberance more redolent of a lion's mane. A good look. Leaving Mr Chilly looking suddenly distinctly more Mr Cool. All that fresh air too took the grey out of the complexion. Transplanting it to where it belonged. Aloft in the flowing locks.

Kevinia couldn't help but notice. And couldn't help but perk up a bit. Yet another perk of his new profession, this distinctly more perky cuddly snuggly stuff. Dear little Annabel couldn't help but notice how the bedroom door appeared to be locked rather more often these days, and couldn't help but be slightly put out. But, Keef reasoned: "A man's gotta do what a man's gotta do". He liked a good western. Among other things.

And now, just as God works in mysterious ways, so too were the ways of Kafka. Kafka-eske indeed was how Keef characterised the changed countenance of his suddenly neighbourly neighbour. All guns blazing no more, the man came in peace. And brought posses of chums in abundance.

Piecing together the social jigsaw, and its miraculous metamorphosis from chaos to harmony, was beyond Keef. And Kevinia. But their cup of happiness overflowed. And old Fallow, in his cups during a barbecue one warm summer night, finally spilled the beans. Not a blazing saddles moment, mind, but they got wind of his game.

"Well, see, it's like this, see. I were never much cop as a bledy farmer, see. Place was too bledy small, see. Worked for my father, and granfer. But I could never make it bledy pay. And all they bledy tractors all over the place. So bledy old and ready for the knacker's yard. Same as me.

"But I took my boots off so I could think clear, see. If I could make the bledy place into one o' they there farm shops. Wi' a garden centre. And one o' they little cafés and gift shops. And all they bledy old knackered buildings turned into bledy holiday lets, that lets me off the hook, see.

"Trouble is, I needed liquidity. I got no bledy money, see, to do the bledy conversion, see. Liquidity, see. That's what I lacked.

"But it was the sea, see, that provided the liquidity. Water, see. That's liquid. Heave they bledy tractors over the cliff and they insurance beggers, they never going to know they were no bledy use anyway."

Wind against tide blasted in Keef's breast. The insurance agent should have grassed the rascal up. But the grass for the postie was so much greener. Ah, how Keef rejoiced in the death of a salesman! And, anyway, old Fallow's next disclosure dissipated any pangs of conscience. Fate had obliged. Stepped in where angels feared to tread. Saved them the trouble.

Somehow the insurance industry had fathomed Fallow's

fallacies. And blacklisted him. So now he had all the buildings. But couldn't run the business. Public liability? He were beggered, and he knew it.

But the Fallow-Kernow fortunes, like the county of whose loins they were the fruit, were not destined for destitution. They were hardy, equipped to adapt to survive. As the incomers would secure the income. Sorting the public liability problem by means of a limited liability company. Which they would run. As partners to old Fallow.

Kevinia had, after all, trained and practised as an accountant before the kids came along. And was now well ready to give it another go. Besides, beside the seaside, as she would now be at the Kernow-Kafka Café and Fallow Farm Garden Centre, she and the marine birds could finally get up close and personal.

In the end, the Kafka's quit the estate where they'd first landed, and moved in to the old milking parlour on Fallow farm instead. Thus trading an uninteresting venue for an uninterrupted sea view.

Increasingly they absorbed the local customs and dress and speech patterns. Binder string would have been de trop, but wooly hats de rigueur. Their faces became more weatherbeaten. And as time went on they'd say, "Where be you to?" with less and less of a trace of mockery.

Old Fallow continued to potter about the old farm for the rest of his days. Providing produce for the shop and rejoicing in being well provided for himself. And Abigail and dear little Annabel eventually inherited the business and passed it on, in time, to their own dear little darlings. To whom the home counties were as remote a part of their heritage as the trees out of which their ancestors had climbed.

Thus did this little corner of this almost annexed field remain forever Kernow. Intruders? The waters closed over their heads. Just like the tractors.

4

Cor-Cor-Cornish
Con-Con-Contrivances

Cor-Cor-Cornelius Cor-Cor-Cornish cornered the market in utter, unutterably undeniable, decency.

To give the word its fullest expression, and the world no possible grounds for reproach, he went so far as to take baths in his underwear. Though even he sometimes smiled at this.

But, essentially, he saw his Role In Life as one of perpetual, almost abject abstinence.

Perhaps something in his infancy had unfavourably affected his emotional progress. Though there was no record of his ever seeing anything nasty in the woodshed. Or anywhere else.

Nonetheless, his b-b-byword was ever "Never push yourself for-for-forward, old b-b-boy. Always make way for the other f-f-fellow."

He oozed charm. From every pore of his diaphanous skin. From every joint in his angular frame. From his prominently chiselled cheekbones to his inexplicably aristocratic ankles.

Unlike his means, he was slender to a fault. To an almost anorexic degree. It's not often you see a stick insect in a bow tie, but there's a first time for everything.

And, as some people lie about their age, some, somehow, do the same about their appearance. And some can even tell porkies about their personality. Sometimes that can be no bad thing. At least, from their point of view.

It wasn't that Cor-Cor-Cornelius didn't love his fellow man. Of the right sort, obviously, not the riff-raff. It was more that he was afraid of him. And the charm kept the chap at bay. It acted as a kind of shield, handy when you haven't got a sword.

Alas, he hadn't got much in the accomplishment department either. No problem with the attributes needed to make him a gentleman. But abilities needed to keep him that way? That was the difficulty.

Genteel poverty can be a runner. Being posh on the dole can't.

Of course, as long as nothing went wrong, and no one got too close, he was safe. But for Cor-Cor-Cornelius, that security sometimes felt as fragile as his own delicately lined forehead.

SCENES, in the earshot of servants or not, would have been as unattractive to him as having a catheter inserted in a mixed ward in an NHS hospital.

Bespoke were his manners. At one with his wardrobe. And his web woven of almost unctuous anxiety to please.

His politesse to excess extended even to Ebenezer Eeewotdoes, at least to his face. Strictly sotto voce, Cor-Cor-Cornelius and his sister Cor-Cor-Cordelia referred to him as Ca-Ca-Caliban. But never in his presence. After all, he did do all the boring bearing of logs into the house. And had never once been heard to say: "There's wood enough within."

All a great comfort to the Cor-Cor-Cornishes. As they would no more have wished to perform so menial a function themselves as perform an appendectomy on their own person. With a blunt butter knife.

Ebenezer, in his turn, blunted many of life's sharper edges for the simpering siblings. Many more than either cared to admit, though both privately acknowledged.

There had been that unfortunate misunderstanding, for example, between Cor-Cor-Cornelius and a certain younger woman. That could so easily have led to a most unfortunate match, culminating in game set and match for her, and cur-cur-curtains for the Cor-Cor-Cornishes. Financially.

Everything about the woman, from her phoney phonetics to the preposterous protruding of her little finger while drinking tea, was suspect.

Unsurprisingly, Cor-Cor-Cordelia was unsure about Cruella Da La-Di-Dah's credentials from the start. But still, she allowed her uncertainties to be undermined by her smitten brother's blindness.

And it wasn't until Ebenezer entrapped the not so good lady into prying in the safe deposit, having first ensured that Cor-Cor-Cornelius was in a darkened corner of the room, that the bedazzled dupe saw the light.

"What is it with they carriage custom, they don't spot a mad mare till she kicks their bledy eyes out," Ebenezer mused, genuinely bemused.

But, as well as a wise man, Ebenezer was a good servant. So he kept his counsel. On this, as on every occasion.

From now on, though, he gave it a bit of extra welly when he ironed the pink paper for Cor-Cor-Cornelius.

Not THE Pink Paper, you understand. Whatever may or may not have taken place on the playing fields of Eton during his time there, display of any kind was vulgarity in Cor-Cor-Cornelius's leather-bound book.

But to the other pink paper, the salmon-shaded one, he accorded biblical status.

"What between the duties expected of one in one's lifetime, and the duties exacted from one after one's death, land has ceased to be either a profit or a pleasure," had been one of the favourite sayings of his austere Aunt Augusta during his childhood. Or was it something he'd read somewhere? He really could not quite recall.

Either way, investments were the W-w-way F-f-forward. F-f-fact.

And f-f-facts of a f-f-financial nature had to be regularly, if discreetly, checked. Hence the persistent perusal of the

Eff-eff-eff Tee. Tedious though the activity eff-eff-effing well was.

But today, and here was the rub, three noughts appeared rubbed out. Three noughts not merely absent, but Not There to an unprecedented degree. On the piece of the page that normally reassured Cor-Cor-Cornelius that a life of anxious but ample idleness was his for all time.

In short, the price of the shares that sheltered Cornelius' c-c-coffers had c-c-crashed. Or so he thought, so hastily had his glance glanced over the crease in the page that Ebenezer Eewotdoes had so unwontedly and unwelcomely ironed into it.

So well, till now, could Cor-Cor-Cornelius afford the magnanimity that comes readily to victors with readies to spare. Unlike for poor people, for whom it's one of the many luxuries they can't afford.

"So how's a f-f-fellow to fl-fl-flourish now?" his mind faltered. Which of his f-f-fellows was to get him out of this ghastly scrape?

"Greater love hath no man than this, that a man should lay down his friends for his life," was something he thought he remembered reading somewhere. Or something like that.

Whatever. He was now even more doggedly, though suddenly very much dog-eat-doggedly, minded to put the other fellow first. Any other fellow, who could be pushed into the pit instead of him.

Far from making him stronger, the Cruella crisis had just

made him more prone to panic. He knew it was his own stupid fault, but owning up did not come easily.

Nor did any kind of solution. "A gentleman does not work for a living," had been a byword in his family for generations. Which works for the upper classes. But not when they're on their uppers.

Forget faith, hope and charity, it was now a matter of beg, borrow or steal. Steeling himself to any of this did not come easily. But in the end nicking his sister's stash seemed favourite.

After all, she did have trust funds of her own. "Enough. I trust," she always said, in her understated, understanding sort of way.

"Trust HER", thought her brother, unfraternally and unkindly, "to have FAR more than she needs. Daddy's little pet. Stinky little squit."

He didn't really mean that. But if you're going to be really mean, the means must justify the ends. So he had to begin by finding reasons for hating the woman.

Hatefully hard, seeing as she'd always treated him so kindly. Well, apart from that time so long ago when she'd told on him, grassed him up, when he was having such a lovely time setting fire to beehives.

So cruel of her, thought the twelve-year-old Cornelius, discreetly overlooking his own behaviour and motives. It was all in the cause of scientific research, he told himself at the time. How else could you find out whether, as swans sing only at the very doorway to death, bees did the same thing?

"Nasty, nasty, nasty, nasty little boy!" his father had raged, unsurprisingly unhappy at his son's behaviour.

"But, but, but but P-p-p-pater . . ." Cornelius had faltered. Comforting himself with cheerful reflections about that predecessor researcher and particular hero of his, Doctor Josef Mengele of the Third Reich. The Angel of Death to his friends.

"After all," he thought to himself, "you can't make an omelette without breaking eggs." Again, a comforting reflection, given its association with that other great icon of his early years, the beloved and world-renowned statesman Joseph Stalin.

Later, he did come to realise, neither of these chaps was quite what they'd been cracked up to be by his prep school history teacher. Who turned out to be a shade eccentric. So much so that he ended his days in Broadmoor. Under the impression, mistaken or otherwise, that he was Vlad the Impaler.

So Cor-Cor-Cornelius did learn to accept that genocide, industrial scale torture, callous disregard of extreme human suffering and mass murder of bees were really not very nice.

But his dad remained unsure about his character. For the rest of his life. Unfairly, perhaps, but understandably. And, such was the convoluted logic of poor cornered Cor-Cor-Cornelius's meandering mind, it was all his sister's fault.

So now it was payback time. Big time. And if you're going to be vile, you need bile. Lots of it. And it amazed him what rancorous reflections came to hand in those tormented insomniac hours under the monogrammed silken sheets.

Cor-Cor-Cordelia was too-too-too much. She HAD too-too-too much. And she jolly well deserved to be relieved of some of the burden. She had had it coming to her. And now she was going to see it going away from her. Masses of it. Subtly, but deftly. And definitely. Today.

"Cor-Cor-Cordelia d-d-DEAREST," he murmured caressively, as he carefully sipped his Earl Grey tea and she did the same with her Lady Grey. (Attention to detail was ever de-de-de rigueur in Cor-Cor-Cornish affairs.)

"I worry", he went on, in his most sorrowfully soothing tone, "that you may have been misled in money matters. And money matters, you know. Or perhaps don't, as you are only a woman after all."

But while he'd got his sister's gender right, he had utterly NOT got the mailed female fist in the voluptuous velvet glove.

All her adult life she'd been protective of her older but woefully not wiser brother. His dissembling disingenuousness cut no ice, as she could see right through him. Though admittedly, his waist being barely wider than his neck made that easier.

She had long suspected that his worldly way of talking masked an utterly unworldly way of thinking. Or, rather, not

73

d

thinking. Cruella had been the clincher. Sisterly love she had in abundance, but she could do tough love too. If she had to.

Florence Nightingale, then. But in a new light. Burning steely bright. Better be the lady with the lamp than the lady and the tramp, she reasoned. As his line of questioning was clearly baited, and she was not prepared to be hooked.

For some reason, though for the life of her she could not fathom what, the bloke was broke. It was obvious.

Of course, they lived together, and she was indeed flush with cash. And was determined to keep it that way. If he'd carelessly lost their combined castle's outer walls, she would keep the keep. Safe and secure. For both of them.

Hence the uncharacteristically uncharitably unloving posture she adopted as her brother began bartering. Badgering. Wheedling. Wondering. Could she, a mere girlie and child in the grown up affairs of men, by the remotest possibility be even the tiniest bit susceptible to the slightest, most minuscule mathematical miscalculation?

"Oh no, d-d-dear," she retorted. "My figures match my figure to perfection. Which is perfection. On this, as on all points, I am firm.

"So, in answer to your next demand, doubtless to be granted untrammelled access to my passwords, memorable facts, security questions, sort codes and account numbers, dear Cor-Cor-Cornelius, you are cor-cor-cordially NOT invited!"

The X Tractor

Once again p-p-poor tor-tor-tortured Cor-Cor-Cornelius and the blessed balm of sleep were total strangers that night. As his mind thrashed in time with his body. About what other sucker he could rip off, seeing as his sister was going to be so typically rotten, spoilt and generally stinky.

He seriously contemplated burying his entire collection of Dinky Toy tractors, lovingly saved in their little boxes since he was too little to need a box for playing cricket, and telling the chaps at Coutts insurance department that some fiendish interloper had made off with them all.

Sad to say, it wasn't his moral compass that steered him away from this course. He was just too scared.

But at one point he did ponder prodding under the mattress on which Ebenezer Eeewotdoes nightly laid his emaciated bones. Though, knowing how little he'd ever paid him, he could easily calculate that the miserable old pauper couldn't possibly have put away anything like enough to be of any use. Unless he'd been doing a spot of drug dealing or gun running on the side. Which did not seem his style.

And yet it WAS old diamond geezer Ebenezer who saved the day. The next day. By forgetting the effing Eff-Tee ironing thing. It just passed clean out of his mind. And the paper he passed to The Master, being less pressed, was less pristine in appearance. Yet, in the other sense of the word, altogether more so.

So as Cor-Cor-Cornelius cast his eyes listlessly over the

miserable lists of mercurial numbers, lo and behold! The Miracle! No mirage! A million!

The noughts were where they should be. All of them.

All, then, was as it should be. As it had always been. In the best of all possible worlds. In the twinkling of an eye.

Eat your heart out, Doctor Pangloss. This called for a celebration. Expiation even. Given the not wholly holy hotbed of emotions he'd harboured regarding his sister. Who, he now aphoristically acknowledged, was the visible personification of absolute perfection. Contrary to his earlier impression.

Thinking about it, he'd been pretty vile about poor old Ebenezer too. Loyal, virtuous, wise and uncomplaining Ebenezer. A credit to his class.

It would no more have occurred to him that this was a patronising proposition than to have traded in his sturdily dependable old typewriter for one of those ghastly co-co-computer things. Denizens as they were of some faraway parallel universe of which he knew nothing.

"If the lower orders cannot set us an example, what is the p-p-possible use of them?" he murmured, smilingly, to himself. Untroubled about whether here was a witticism he'd thought up for himself for once. Or not.

Anyway, come Christmas, the chap was going to get, by way of bumper bonus, his own telephone line installed in his own room. So when he rang his ancient and eighty per cent deaf mother he could bellow about her beleaguered bodily functions without the currently obligatory audience of Cor-Cor-Cornishes. Nice for him. And for them too, as it happens. Especially at mealtimes.

In the event, Ebenezer would have preferred one o' they there smartphones with Internet access, a twenty megapixel camera and all the latest apps. But such a concept would have been as alien to Cor-Cor-Cornelius as little green men popping over from Mars.

In her turn, Cor-Cor-Cordelia would have preferred some explanation, logical or otherwise, of her brother's uber bipolar mood swing. But that prospect was as remote as recognition that his attitude to women would not have been out of place in the court of King Canute. Or the lair of King Kong.

Instead she was content with the conviviality of a nice Gin and It. Well, several, as it turned out. Shaken, stirred and served with verve by Ebenezer. And shared with the dear old chap. The Cor-Cor-Cornishes half wondered in their half cut cups whether to share with him the Caliban gag too. But gagged themselves in the end. Which was probably for the best.

Instead, Cor-Cor-Cornelius contemplated the confluence of events behind this splendidly sociable soirée. In his mind he played out the twists and turns. The agonies and the ecstasies. Rehearsing, reworking, refining his script till it was perfection.

At last, as confusingly as it would have been to cinema

audiences if all they'd heard in *Gone With the Wind* was: "Frankly my dear, I don't give a damn," he gave them all they were going to get.

"All's well that ends well." That was it. The end. Finito.

He slumped back in his handsome horsehair-stuffed gentleman's brown leather armchair, unruffled by any untoward uncertainties. HAD someone written a play of that name? If so, who?

Aw, hell. Who gives a damn?

5

Lord Haw-Haw Humbled

The lad's nails shimmered in the mid-morning sun. He considered them appraisingly. Appreciatively. Perhaps a shade smugly.

Maybe he was that kind of guy.

Or maybe a man on the run. From that run of bad luck begun when he was from his mother's womb untimely ripped. Bereft of her scent. Sent into exile. Descent into hell, it felt like. Seeing as he was only five at the time.

English public schools. Once the bastions of brutality and squalor and backbone of the British Empire, don't you know? Funny how it didn't last. Like the early Christian church, on account of its fondness for martyrdom, and total immersion at baptisms.

Total immersion in the communal cold bath was the ritually nasty start to the day where lucky little Horace-Horatio Haw-Haw Cornish received his start in life.

Definitely more costly than cosy. Money well spent? Discuss.

Such boarding establishments have now mostly reined back on the old sport-spawned savagery, and noticed that passing exams can have its compensations. And that sadomasochism is not all that it's cracked up to be.

But Horace-Horatio's cathedral of culture prided itself on tried and tested traditionalism. The Combined Cadet Force still universally referred to as the Officer Training Corps. Even though the name was changed, to keep up with the times, in 1948.

So, following sound Darwinian principles, our hero became a Regimental Sergeant Major, and proved himself rugged on the rugger pitch, and cracking at cricket. Shame he was such a farce in the classroom. Fast track to nowhere.

His final academic achievement amounted to two borderline passes. In carpentry and divinity. In a moment of divine inspiration, the careers officer suggested he become an undertaker. Dead funny, but didn't quite measure up to expectations.

And for some reason, Horace-Horatio was now discovering, there didn't seem much call in the real world for his school skills. Shouting surprisingly loudly, running surprisingly fast, and inflicting extreme violence on spherical and airship-shaped leather balls.

The leathery psychic skin he'd grown during those interminable unhappy years was, likewise, less of a hit nowadays. Too much mojo in his manner, perhaps. Bombastic? Bumptious? Fractious? And, frankly, infuriating. Quite a cocktail. Ideal for funerals. Preferably, one's own.

All that money the parents had paid out. Yet so little access during term time daytimes to that most basic of commodities, soap. No wonder he so valued his fastidious finger ends now. He'd waited long enough.

Still, his parents hadn't had to wait too long before getting the boy out of their hair and on with their lives. School fees? Worth every penny.

He looked every inch the part at least. Tall and slender, with lashings of flaxen hair falling gracefully over his frank and unfurrowed forehead. Against that, he had the habit of drumming his fingers on any available surface. Fine old military tattoos. Both imperial, and, to the onlooker, imperious.

But was there, Brogan-Brietta Tre-Pen-Tre-Pentree wondered, a shadow of sadness etched in the eyes? In build, and temperament if crossed, she was short and sharp. Her trim little form of a piece with the neat little nose and chin. Pointed, like the questions she'd pose. Especially of poseurs. Or anyone at all suspect.

Suspect? In his opening gambit at the We Will Rock You eating establishment, Horace-Horatio made Guy Fawkes seem the soul of innocence. Hands outstretched, eyes open wide: "Mass murderer? Moi? What gunpowder?"

Whatever, Horace-Horatio's social implosion mission began thus: "Air, I sair, let's have a rynde of taist". Bad taste compounded by the studied pause for one final pre-conversation cuticle inspection. They looked good, and he sounded it, he thought. She didn't.

Brogan-Brietta was Definitely Cornish. Born and bred. Complexion and intonation to match. And softly spoken contemplative manner that masked her mastery of matters analytical. Even the really impossible stuff.

She only helped out at her cousin's café in the summer by way of a break from her university studies. Arguably, anyone writing a PhD thesis in cognitive-existential psychology deserves a break.

And a break, or better still multiple fractures to legs and spine, suddenly seemed too good for this sprawling, drawling lout. A less than rational response. But addressing her as an inferior species, a mere woman, mere serving-wench even? Excuse MOI!

Actually, he rather liked the look of her. He could read the intelligence in her eyes, and was quite seriously scared of it. He felt his inner temperature rising. The military march broke into a charge, as he deployed his deadliest defensive weaponry. About as useful, however, as a water cannon against a battleship.

Still, it was the best he could do. Like the patrician patois. Which he perfectly well knew was as unfathomable to natives as, say, phenomenological intersubjectivity. A topic on which it happened that Brogan-Brietta was something of an expert.

She was also pretty good at pretension deflation. You come up against all sorts at universities that cater for PhD students. And, to the cognoscenti, "Air, I sair, let's have a rynde of taist" easily translates into: "Oh, I say, let's have a round of toast." Piece of cake, as it were.

Still, there remained the question of whether to unleash her inner psychopath, in all its primordial glory, or to mother him in some way. Putting him over her knee and spanking him would do for starters. They could kiss and make up later.

But what he said next inclined him less towards the balm of the bosom than getting his neck wrung. Or his skull stove in with pointed sticks. Or being torn limb from limb or flayed alive. Or having his liver pecked out by large, unpleasant birds of prey.

"Nigh look haaar," he intoned insidiously, at the same time running his hand irksomely gracefully through his tousled hair. "You look a game sort of lass. Why not take a turn with me and the lads tonight for a little shindig we've got planned. Plenty of hooch and a bit of hokey cokey, what? Bit of slap and tickle, eh?"

"Now look here," she was about to translate. And elaborate: "You can slap your tickle right up your hokey cokey, unctuous little upstart."

But she said nothing of the kind. What a piece of work is man. How noble in reason. How infinite in faculties. But how weirdly illogical half the time. And the women can be worse.

Or maybe it's just where wind hits tide. Always a spot of turbulence. Sometimes terminal. They say old fishermen never die. They're lying.

But should Brogan-Brietta take this lying down? And if so, why? Maybe it was that scintilla of sadness she'd read in his eyes. Surely not that rather pretty little kiss curl that so delicately delineated itself across his brow? Absolutely not. In his dreams.

On balance, the scales WERE against it. But in the kaleidoscope of human emotion there might have been a flicker. She knew about such inner conflicts. Indeed, had had papers published on the subject. But it's so much easier to read other people than oneself.

And Horace-Horatio did seem something of a case study. Maybe an archetype of victimhood. Albeit an amazingly annoying one.

Anyway, her mouth said yes, though her eyes implied an outstanding spanking. For the both of them. Still, her reason resolved to take the lad in hand and hand him a mirror, that he might see himself as others saw him. Metaphorically speaking.

The evening came, and they went, to the sand dunes. There to meet with . . . Horace-Horatio's horrible gaggle of chums. Collectively, a cacophony. As discordant as they were disagreeable. And so loud.

And, when assembled, so indistinguishable from one another. One's charming little terrier can be so sweet, loving and docile at home. And so tolerant of the baby. But get it out with other dogs and it's the three-headed Hound of Hades. Odd, that.

Likewise, Horace-Horatio, somehow vulnerable for all his insouciance at the café, now reverted to type with a peculiar vengeance. More sinned against than sinning, maybe. Hitler doubtless had disagreeable experiences in his formative years. But you can go off people.

As the night wore on and the boys bored on, ever more boorish and less coherent, there grew on our hero a dim but sinking awareness that the little filly he thought he'd so skillfully ensnared was not merely all she had seemed, but a lot more besides.

His intermittent asides to her, to the effect that she looked rather dainty with her dear little pigtails and slinky little slacks, seemed not to have the desired effect. Something in her body language, reminiscent of an avenging fury on a bad night out, provided a clue.

She had already pressed the mental search button and alighted on grand old Granny Gertie. The last and only other person she had ever heard refer to slacks, and that disparagingly. A garment, she explained, precursor to jeans, that women had been allowed to wear on the golf links but not in the members' dining room.

"Despicable breed, the world over, the petit bourgeoisie," she added acidly. "Chairman Mao was on to something, marching his lot to death."

Never knowingly understated, Granny Gertie deployed enormous earrings, pince-nez and an extravagantly long silver cigarette holder as an updated version of the sword and buckler. Formative in Brogan-Brietta's development and formidable in academia, she was ever on the lookout for orthodoxies. To dash to the ground, like so many broken mirrors, in a thousand shattered shards.

Brogan-Brietta sometimes asked herself what had possessed her in that moment of adolescent madness to have tattooed on her left forearm: "All you need is love . . ." And on the right: ". . . And a great set of wheels." Then she would look at Granny and know she need look no further.

What she was minded now, but couldn't muster the energy to actually say, would have enlightened Horace-Horatio. "Shame the stone from under which you crawled didn't crush you, you patronising, sexist, dog-brained brat. And where DID you get that ridiculous cravat?"

Poor Brogan-Brietta. For her, an entertaining evening included an interesting interchange of ideas. Or at least some kind of cerebral contact. Instead, an interminable tract of time loomed. In the clone zone. For conversation, read banter. Facile at best. And all those idiotic jokes. She began to wonder whether it was possible to actually die of boredom.

Eventually, as the boys broke into song for the umpteenth time, ending each stanza with "up school, up school, up school" she could stand it no longer. Under cover of the moonless blackness and their self-congratulatory, back-slapping guffaws, she silently slipped away.

But slipping that night was her downfall. The dunes were treacherous when you really could see nothing. So she was in no position to detect the presence of the random, rust ridden old tractor that, unaccountably found itself half buried in the sand with wickedly sticky-out bits everywhere to trap the unwary traveller.

She wondered, fleetingly as she went down, what kind of farmer would be so careless as to just abandon a tractor at the bottom of a cliff like that, and not mind about the money.

Having a brain the size of a giant's is, seemingly, not always proof against the naïve simplicity of a tiny child. Any more than expertise in neuropsychological methodology and computational cognitivism provide protection from a broken ankle. Like "I think therefore I am." No comfort when you've got piles.

Later, much later, blearily impervious to all but a giddy feeling of self-satisfaction and a slight desire to be sick, the Haw-Haw horde heaved itself to its calf-leather clad feet. All recall stalled. A stranger in their midst. What stranger? Vanished. Really?

Happily, however, Horace-Horatio's benumbed senses showed signs of life after death. As dawn broke, along with awareness that the grand seduction scene hadn't quite gone

as planned, he broke away from his chums and into a trot. He could detect a distant whimper in the air, and a faint gnawing at his mental entrails.

"By golly! The filly! She had her fill of us and slithered! Whither?" The preliminary symptom of a slight headache turned into a definite diagnosis of brain fever, now that he was clearly hearing cries of pain. Clearly mingled with expressions of exasperation.

Propriety precludes precision about her choice of words. Suffice it to say the boys' parentage came into question. There was a paraphrasing of the biblical injunction to go forth and multiply. And a variety of references to bodily bits. Male, and female.

It was tempting, therefore, for Horace-Horatio to stand on his dignity. But with Brogan-Brietta unable to stand at all that would hardly have been good form.

So instead he Did the Decent Thing. The Mr Darcy thing. Almost. He got her out of the dunes and into an ambulance.

But what next? In vain did he consult his confederates Smithers and Sticcers about the way forward with the damsel in distress, who had seemed more inclined to strike him than be struck on him. One old chum prescribed more cold baths and bromide in his tea, and the other pointed out there were plenty more natives in the jungle, old boy.

Thus did Horace-Horatio arrive at the foothills of the mountain he was about to climb. The realisation that these boyhood buddies might be pukka on the parade ground, or fun in the scrum, but as much use anywhere else as a five-legged headless horse.

So he broke ranks, the habits of a lifetime, and the bank. He went all the way to Truro to see the lady in hospital. In London all those nice little black buses were always there at your service. Here he had to fork out for some ramshackle charabanc trading as the local taxi service, and the driver's rustic, incomprehensible prattle.

In fairness, the taxi was a perfectly self-respecting Mondeo, only mildly mouldy and, by Cornish standards, relatively unscathed. A credit to the county. And the driver, who had to put bread on the table somehow, was a published poet. From Pontefract, in point of fact.

He was intensely proud of his northern roots, and a great fan of Shelley, Keats and Byron. And, as is so often the way with gentlemen of both his professions, he had something to tell the world. Or, failing that, anything within earshot.

Our hero hit Truro with a head jumbled and benumbed with he knew not what. Some mediaeval king somewhere. With a club foot, was it? Or did he get murdered? Or drowned, this Richard bloke? Perhaps over a weekend. Or was that when he invented a monster? Horace-Horatio wished he'd travelled in the boot.

And all this when he was trying so hard to marshal his thoughts for the great leap forward. Still, never say die, his courage remained screwed to the sticking place. The order to fix bayonets and attack, furiously finger-drummed on the hospital inquiry desk, helped steady his nerves.

The flowers were the easy bit. He'd given them to his mother every birthday, which happened to fall in school holidays. She always said: "Sweet, darling boy. I'll pop them into a vase." And always didn't. Still, the maid made good use of them.

But, bouquets aside, the hard bit was the new beginning. In the beginning was the word. And the word was "sorry". Doesn't take a second to say. Feeling it takes longer. A bit like a kitten. Not just for Christmas.

"Air, my dare," he began unpromisingly, though better was to come: "I'm so frightfully, dreadfully, preternaturally . . . SORRY."

He'd even borrowed a dictionary to look up the meaning of the word "preternatural". Because he could not be sure if it meant frightfully, dreadfully, desperately only with knobs on, or was something to do with a chain of French fast food restaurants.

And it didn't stop there, this mother of all mea culpas. "Air my dare," he resumed, as verbal equivalent to clearing one's throat or spitting on the pavement, "the fact is me and my chums really were the most downright bores and cads. All night. Unforgivable. Unspeakable. UNGENTLEMANLY.

"So, er, sorry," he concluded. Lamely. Which was really rather more her thing than his that day, given her fifty per cent deficiency in the working leg department.

But he had made his point. And it had struck home. Brogan-Brietta was awestruck. Knowing too much about how other people's minds work can leave you baffled by your own. As she was, at that moment. Utterly.

The flowers were a welcome distraction. A veil under which to conceal her confusion. As well as a welcome embellishment to the ward. National health hospitals these days do, after all, need all the help they can get. Besides, putting them in water was a handy reminder of the quality of mercy. Dropping, as it does, like the gentle rain from heaven.

She'd had twenty-four hours to collect her thoughts. To recognise that her brain bore favourable comparison to that of the disgusting little rat who'd borne her thither. Hers being planet sized, his definitely more redolent of a rodent's.

But now he sat before her, pliant and supplicant, with his head bowed. Did he not know that posture showed off his kiss curl to even better advantage? How dare he, the brute?

The truth is, he didn't. Not the foggiest. At school, Matron was so enveloped in starch the Angel Gabriel would have failed to move her. And mother? So silken in dress and tone. Too ethereal to notice. To even be there, when he needed her.

And that was it. Horace-Horatio had never known woman. There the nurses, of course, in the rather soignée private nursing home where he was born. But they didn't count. How could they? He wasn't on speaking terms with the world at the time.

So all he knew of talking to ladies was drawn from dialogue in the rather dreadful and dangerously dated novels he'd read in his pre-pubescent years. Before the prospect of captaincy in every conceivable school team consumed his every waking moment.

"By George, you're a handsome piece of work," he suddenly opined. Then went on, warming to his theme: "The devil you are, now I come to get a good look at you, in that charming frock. Charming, my dear. Quite charming." All he needed, to complete the effect, was a monocle and waxed moustache. The ensemble rounded off by a pot belly and a starched shirt front.

Brogan-Brietta, not normally short of a word or two, or twenty thousand when needed, just gaped at him. Dumbstruck.

"Air, I sair," he concluded, suddenly subdued: "Frightfully sorry. Dashed impertinent of a chap. Should hold me horses. Bit carried away, dammit. Er, sorry and all that." Gone was the well-tempered tattoo now, as the fretful finger ends sadly sounded the retreat. Or was it the last post?

Like the high-pitched screech of some well-heeled ladies, whose voices are only audible to bats, the behavioural and speech patterns emitted by Horace-Horatio seemed only decipherable by aliens. Creatures whose interest in humans is purely anthropological.

Brogan-Brietta had studied specimens in her time. But nothing in her seven years in tertiary education had prepared her for this. Nor in her childhood down the farm. And nor in adolescence spent working at everything from ski resorts to kibbutzim. Was the bloke just barmy?

Balmy days followed, however. Horace-Horatio paid homage to the laid up lady, visiting her every morning, plying her with every bloom he could find, and listening. And gradually, under her benign and patient tutelage, learning the language of life.

As a pupil, she found him surprisingly apt. And, as a companion, surprisingly amusing, in time. A bit of a puppy of course, but every bit as pretty. And such fun to teach.

No. There was no romance. Was never going to be. But, and maybe even the flowers played their part, there was a blossoming. An understanding. Useful for Brogan-Brietta as a scientist. Never to discount the incalculable. No matter how inscrutable. Or just plain weird.

Years later, when she was married and a mother, as well as a Professor, she would look back fondly on this interlude. This intimacy of opposing poles. The tender nurturing of a tender shoot.

And Horace-Horatio? Holidays over, he would write regularly to his Cornish mentor and first true friend. Tell her of the studies he'd taken up to fill the gaps in his education. Not so much gaps, he later conceded, as one vast void. A flapping marquee marked "learning". With nothing in it at all.

But he wasn't as stupid as he'd always imagined. And he had the time. And his parents had the money. And now he did live at home. It was payback time.

e

6

The Cause of True Love

Micky Fabb was the axeman par excellence. Loud, louche, lanky and swanky. Sweatily swaggering from gig to gig. Thus defying the rule that while a lady merely glows, a gentleman perspires. Leaving it to horses to sweat. Singing yourself hoarse does make you hot. Fact.

On stage and off it, Mickey's Fender agenda surrendered to no man. Or woman. He was born under an ancient oak, man. Under Aquarius, man. At Glastonbury, man. He was that romantic ruin. Though more alpha male than holy grail. On the plectrum spectrum.

All lies, of course. He was actually born under an Artex ceiling in Surbiton. More suburban than urban spaceman. So not cool that not a soul was allowed to know. In Cornwall, where he knew no one, he could be anyone. Which was much better. So much more not not cool.

Here he could be fixed, barren, masculine and dry.

Aquarian to his aquiline nose. To the split ends of his huge hair. A shade peroxide, perhaps, but masses of it. The hell with quality, quantity counts. Forget that glib, soi-disant axiom about less being more. More IS more. Fact. Get used to it. And forget all that nonsense about content too. Just go for the packaging.

And check out the fretted fingertips in the rockabilly boogie bits. He was that muso with a muse. And no ties. No strings attached. Apart from to his guitar. Obviously.

Music was the one lingering link between the Micky Fabb of fame and fortune, and the Humfrey Shufflebum of his youth. Trained as a choirboy and a talented organist, a sensitive soul. And so fond of his pet pussycats, Peaches and Cream. Bit of a girlie really.

And so shy and retiring. Till pater got retired. Forcibly.

When mater made off with a missionary, Reverend Rufus Shufflebum confided in a married parishioner that she'd run off to the West Indies.

"Jamaica?" the woman wondered.

"No, she went of her own accord," he replied. No, he really did say that. Honestly. He was that unworldly.

And that unwise, when this devout personage, secretly devoted to him for years, got her frock off. This bereft man, urgently seeking solace, got his rocks off. And, when the word got out, he was out. Just like the lady. Defrocked.

So, wife, roof and career caved in, he did the only logical thing. Vowed never to visit the hairdresser again, grew an implausibly plonkerly bushy beard, went to Wales, and formed a druidic sect in a cave. As you do.

And what could Humfrey do? Shack up with Peaches and Cream at Battersea Cats' home? His own having gone with his father's living. No, that would never work. For a start he had not enough legs to qualify for sanctuary. And was rubbish at purring.

But, what a friend he had in Jesus. Or verging on it. Dad's ex-verger had noticed that, leading the singing and swopping organ for electric guitar, Humfrey got hot licks. This was hardly a hotline to heaven. But it did have the effect of making the happy clappy claptrap suddenly sound almost like music. God, whatever next?

What next? The stage. The Surbiton Operatic Dramatic society, SODS for short, was doing a rock musical and wanted someone to play the rock star. So the verger put him up for the part. In return for putting him up. SODS law, so to speak.

He was a smash hit. And even got smashed on the closing night, for the first time in his life. This was hardly his style. Nor the verger's, who kicked him out. He gave him the keys to his beat up old Volkswagen camper van and told him to decamp. Somewhere east of Eden. Or west. Sodom would do nicely.

"Sod'im," said the suddenly worldly Humfrey. "It's all SODS fault." It was all so out of character for him. But so IN character for the rock star he'd just played. To such plaudits.

So here lay his future. A wandering minstrel I. With a roving eye. Why not? He picked up the pussycats and got well west before the camper conked. Fair enough, it was far enough. Brick up the wheels and may SODS will be done. In Cornwall as it was in Surbiton.

"Hell, man. Home is where I hang my hat," he drawled. More Mickey Spillane than Micky Fabb. But insincerity is how we multiply our personalities. Ask any politician.

Anyway, the ex-honourable member for Surbiton was now the dishonourable dude from Glastonbury, strutting and fretting from gig to gig. But under it all still the same soppy old softie. Bless 'im.

He was that walking shadow. That rather brilliant player. And if an actor can manifest murderer Macbeth then go home to a nice cup of tea, he could play madcap Micky and go home to his nice little kitties. Siamese, if you please. Siamese if you don't please. Obvious who wore the trousers in that household. Not him.

But he had fangs. Reserved for the fans. And the more he hissed and spat, the more the groupies groped. And with the music so retro, so abstract, so, hey man, swoony, they just seemed to waft out of a hippy dippy clone zone. Scenic, yes. But seen one, seen 'em all.

Period skirts, period vocabulary, past caring capes, flakily flared strides, and seriously silly sunglasses. Thus was the ensemble assembled. To the untrained observer it might have seemed odd how, when they were all so free, man, so

enlightened and so different that they all always thought the same things. Perhaps it was the cosmos, man? Yerright.

All so pagan, they were. Though you wonder whether they could have filled half a page of foolscap with what they thought paganism was. Without resorting to ludicrously large handwriting. Though it would have seemed a bit below the low-slung wide-buckled diamante-studded belt to ask them to try.

What mattered was that they were protected by witchcraft. That much was obvious. It said so on posters, stickers, dream catchers, fridge magnets and bongs all over their homes. Their "pads", as they called them.

And the real-life pads on the brakes of their crumbling, rust-ridden, unreal old wheels needed all the breaks they could get. Depress the middle pedal and not much happens. Which is not such a problem in Holland. But in Cornwall, decidedly depressing.

But, letting that pass, as the days generally did, dreamily, for most of them most of the time, Ariel-Oceana Pendragon-Pendrogget really was a bit different. From most other folk. And from the rest of the coven. And from the Bertha of her birth.

Sad to relate, some unfortunate souls actually do get baptized Bertha. A hundred years ago it happened more often. These days, generally only if the dominant parent is a callous bully bent on the child's social suicide. A fast track to the Samaritans.

Step forward Elijah Tannker. Solicitor by trade, lay preacher by predilection. Of the worst sort. His sermons sated with quivering brethren Old Testament mumbo-jumbo. Memorable, mesmeric and merciless. Not exactly a glass of sherry before the Sunday roast.

Picture poor Bertha Tannker's tormented infancy, then. And her adolescence. How many different ways are there, for god's sake, of putting down people who think they're the first to ever notice that Bertha Tannker is a funny name? Well, face it. It is.

Happily, the otherwise hapless Bertha was bright. So she was able to escape from despicable Dad and rubbish role model Mum. To another universe. University. Upcountry.

There she luxuriated over the line: "What's in a name? That which we call a rose by any other name would smell as sweet." She also discovered that, when originally performed at the Globe, it got a good belly laugh. Because of the neighbouring Rose Theatre's smelly drains.

She learned lots. And came back to the other end of Cornwall with no fetters. Just letters. Loads of them, after her name. Which, like Humfrey Shufflebum, got the boot. Along with the identity father forced her to wear like a crown of thorns. She could have crowned the old devil.

Mrs Angryperson she was, to the soles of her ankle boots. Which was why joining the hippie drippy set suited her splendidly, given the contempt in which her hate-sated pater held such people. Actually, he spat at anyone who wasn't like him. But them especially. Their so-called religion? A stairway to hell.

It was heavenly, then, for ex-Bertha, joining the club. Albeit, covertly in the coven, only as an affiliate member. To cover her discreetly achieving tracks, she'd say, when off to London to confer with colleagues, in the course of her richly remunerative research career, that she was off to raves. Man.

Keener eyed coven members, in the brief interludes between shelf stacking shifts and mind-enhancing spliffs, noticed that this woman who flaunted the name Ariel-Oceana like Imelda Marcos' shoe collection, didn't always conform to the dress code. Indeed, she seemed sometimes more Gucci than grunge. But, hey man, they were so free. Man.

Besides, she had such striking eyebrows, which she'd inherited from her father. Though in his case they were more glower than flower power. In the name of Our Father, he could even make the hairs in his nostrils bristle. This was disgusting, but deadly.

By rights, Micky Fabb should have been her deadly enemy too. So grossly gargantuan. So male. So macho. So much the monster she so despised. The visible personification of absolute abortion material.

But her delicately turned up little nose, so not stuffed with superfluous follicular baggage, could discern discrete distinctions in the cow-poo-plastered pastures of Cornwall. As well as in parfumerie at Harrods.

And, just as she was more angular than angelic in build, so she fell to wondering if the fellow didn't have an angle to him. Maybe masking his inner angel. Was there something, sometimes, wistful in his eye? Or was that just wishful thinking?

Then again she was a Paganini person. A bit of a violin virtuoso in her own right. And well aware that, just like Micky Fabb, Nicky Pag also played guitar. Not a lot of people know that. George Best was also rather fond of cricket. Not a lot of people know that either.

But, more to the point, was there a point at which Micky's mysterious musicality harmonised with her own inner rhythms? Maybe music can speak louder than manners. And, oh yes, he did loud all right. His amps generally generating enough watts to flatten a wattle and daub hut at a hundred paces.

Ariel-Oceana, sensible lady that she was, opted for a quiet night to check him out. And, creeping up on the camper, she distinctly heard the sound of sighing. Like a furnace. Wouldn't it be funny, she thought, if even now he's writing a woeful ballad, to his mistress' eyebrow. But on balance, she concluded, this was not very likely.

However, he was indeed doing just that. And flinging away draft after dratted draft of mawkish muck in praise of her very own fabulously fluted facial furry bits. It's hard being a bard. Though Peaches and Cream, purring playfully and conspiratorially, just thought he was being silly.

And maybe he was, a bit, when Ms Pendragon-Pendrogget put in her appearance. Or maybe he was too proud. Or shy. Or just head over heels in love. Whatever, he concealed the crumpled poetic relics and jauntily offered her a joint. Which she declined.

Still, she'd made her point, just by popping by. And his discomfiture did something to diminish his disguise. Seeing as, out and about, he had more front than her favourite corner shop. DEAR old Harrods. And maybe this puffed up posturing poseur also stored all the perfumes of Arabia. Somewhere.

There was no need to rush, though. This was, after all, Cornwall. Do it dreckly and it seems like you're rushing things.

Micky Fabb forlornly wished otherwise. In affairs of the heart, the ghost of Humfrey haunted him. All that shy sensitivity, so safely locked away till now, almost racked the riffs out of him. It made him come over all unnecessary, poor dear.

But the show must go on, and the mask made to fit once again. Now, though, when Ariel-Oceana showed up at gigs he was more Wizard of Oz than whizz on the fizz. He knew it. She knew it. And, though nothing was said, they were already on the yellow brick road.

The right turning at the right juncture came when Farmer Peregrine Proper-Cornish obligingly blundered out of Chapter One of this book and into theirs. It was only a matter of time, given that he only lived round the corner.

Mathematical genius as he had demonstrated himself to be, he still hadn't quite got the hang of making one to sixteen add up. On the Massey Ferguson gearbox. So losing control, not of his temper but of his machinery, was a bit of a Peregrine thing.

And, at the end of one particularly long and not very gay day in the wheat fields, the tractor became intractable. Going round and round in at once convergent and concentric circles. Very fast. Leaving tracks, traces rather, very like the curvilinear creations bestowed on humans by aliens, man.

Discovery of the crop circle, to circles such as those peopled by such as Ariel-Oceana, was food and drink. Ambrosia and nectar. Spiritually, man.

Their lives, so often conducted as some kind of pensive but pointless pilgrimage, now had a Definite Purpose. Here was Definite Proof. Definitely. So by day and by night they paid homage at this extraterrestrial shrine. Wandering wonderingly among its arcane, Arcadian, arcades.

It was like, well like, like some really cool divine force had taken some heavenly magic, like, thing, like some magic flying, hey, man, tractor. And just dropped bits all round everywhere. Like, maybe, like jettisoned fuel tanks. You need loads of them, man, when you've come all the way from, like, Mars. Or the sun. Or the intergalactic indeterminate interface. Or somewhere.

But how to communicate with the communicators? The little green men, or whatever they were, who flew the spaceship that created the pattern that confirmed the conspiracies that entranced them all.

How else but through music? And who else but Micky Fabb to play it?

As it happens, he'd heard the folk down the pub having a good laugh, both at Proper-Cornish's convulsions, and at the hippies' hopeless naiveté. They thought they'd seen the light? Well, praise be.

But there's no business like show business. OK, they do get the applause, but they are paid for what they do. So Micky was not going to disappoint. A gig's a gig, and cigs cost. The same as Peaches and Cream's cream.

Ariel-Oceana too was in on the Peregrine Proper-Cornish secret. As she had as much an ear for gossip as eye for Micky's elusive charms.

Thus, on Apocalypse Night, when the music was to invoke the spirits and the mother of all close encounters was at hand, there was an inner circle within the crop circle. A secret society. A masonry. Between those besotted beauties. More starry eyed than star crossed, as luck would have it.

Late, very late, the last echoes of the last haunting melody melted into the ether, the joss-sticks flickered into non-existence, and the hippies nursed sore mouth muscles from murmuring ommm for so long. And still the spacemen, annoyingly, failed to put in an appearance.

Still, love did. A close encounter made in heaven. In that glint in their eyes of mutual recognition, that unspoken admission of adoration. Gently caressive. Conducive to joy.

Besides, there was the sheer hilarity of the occasion. The crestfallen look on hippie faces. So forlorn. So woebegone little child when cruel mummy takes the toys away. You'd need a heart of stone not to laugh out loud.

And happy Micky and walking-on-air Ariel certainly did that. As the puzzled hippies softly melted away, like dewdrops in the morning sun. Or grumpy old men when the telly packs up. Infernal thing. Always going wrong.

But with things going so right for our bedazzled beauties, was this the moment? The moment critique, ripe for blossoming? The twin entwining of body and soul? Or at least body? There and then?

In the event, no. They both needed space to embrace this brave new world, so peopled with such goodly creatures. To consider all things between heaven and earth, and all they'd dreamed of in their philosophies. Anyway, they were knackered.

"Tomorrow," she murmured.

"And tomorrow," he sighed.

And tomorrow came to pass. And he came to hers. For some reason, armed with the acoustic. So fearless and euphoric only yesterday, so fretfully unsure of himself today, The instrument slung over his shoulder like a spear. His security. Or, silly baby that he was, his security blanket.

His insecurity intensified at the panoply of delicacy before him as he crossed the threshold. It the old days he'd have crossed himself. It was all so set off with the scent of gardenia. Ubiquitous, and unnerving. More soignée than swoony, this gaff. No place for the likes of him.

Anyway, who was he? No great fan of the brat with the Strat, admittedly. But at least, strutting in those borrowed plumes, he could make his entrances and his exits. Besides, who had wooed the lady? And won her? Not shy, shuffling Humfrey, that was sure. Gosh, he was such a fibber-fox. And such a weasel.

Sunk in these deliberations and Ariel-Oceana's salmon-pink chesterfield, he stared listlessly at the violin and sheet music, open on the stand. And catching the direction both of his gaze and maybe his thought, she spoke decisively. Almost imperiously.

"Well, come on. Get it out then."

A rude awakening from a rueful reverie. Extremely rude, actually. He blushed to his roots. And beyond. Suddenly so not cool his face burned purple. Which was not a good look with the blonde. But as she picked up the fiddle he picked up her drift. And finally got it out. Of the gig bag, excuse me.

She played Paganini. And on his heartstrings. Taut, they were, to bursting. Micky's? Humfrey's? And what about the cats? All this catgut and scrapey scoured the seams of his being. But the musical phraseology was fun. And, the notation noted, his fingers twitched.

Her performance was exemplary. His, extempore. The effect, excellent. Where baroque meets rock. Where Micky meets Humfrey. And Ariel-Oceana met the both of them. Quite a ménage. Though Bertha was NOT included. This was a matter of mere modesty. A woman must preserve her mystery, after all.

But the barriers were broken, for all time. And point counter point perfected, at least in four-four, five-four and six-eight. They even kept the tempo in their talk.

"Music's the food of love," he pointed out.

"So play on, give me excess of it," she countered. And nothing succeeds like excess. With their shared shock of blonde locks, so daringly dishevelled, this was love among the haystacks. Big style.

So they got it together. The camper got dumped, they got the paternal ex-Rev to perform some impenetrably Welsh blessing, and the hippies got invited.

It helped heal the dear creatures' spiritual wounds so spitefully inflicted by absent aliens. This cave-dwelling beardy-weirdy a comforting second best. Almost Merlin. And rather a sweetie.

And the pussies found the new sleeping arrangements altogether to their liking. No identity problems for Peaches and Cream. Comfort and style cats, thank you very much. Born to the Ritz. Not the rust bucket.

7

Born-Agains Reborn

The Reverend Gargoyle Buhmboil was used to looking through a glass darkly. As a child, he thought as a child, but when he became a man he put away childish things. Or tried to. Though he did find his adult infirmity infantile in the extreme. As well as painful, when trying to sit for any length of time.

It made no odds how often, or how devoutly, he implored dear old Pater Noster to deliver us from evil, it never made any difference. Obviously, kneeling helped. But, sedentary posture resumed, the problem of his rear reared its horrid head again. Immediately.

So well he knew that the most terrifying words in the English language for any god-fearing fellow should really be "hellfire and brimstone". But for him, alas, they were trumped by "take a pew".

But it was not just the posterior pustules that took the

shine out of his life. It was also his dwindlingly diminutive congregation. So much for Our Father's power and glory lasting forever and ever. That may be so up there. But it's a bit different down here. And a bit worse every year.

At the onset of each winter, old Doctor Hip-Hip-Hippocrates down at the surgery used to cheerily rub his hands together and say: "Hip-hip hooray! Another good clear-out!"

It was all very well for him, with retirement just round the corner, to have a workload diminishing with his client base. But the reverse for the Reverend, who could only lament God's partiality for fleecing him of his flock to make up HIS numbers in heaven. From a strictly earthly perspective, a bit tight of him.

Time was, before Gargoyle's time, when devout human stock would be topped up each year. With a transfusion of younger blood. But, sadly, in the capacious body of earthly society, denominational devotees were becoming a vestigial organ. Like the appendix. Or, as any good feminist will tell you, the male brain.

So well he remembered earlier and happier times, at the theology knowledge college, when he prophesied his coming to a sleepy little village where he would minister to a select but sturdy little flock. He would behold his world, and, behold! He would find it good.

He would pull his portly person up at the pulpit to its full five feet five inches, benignly twinkle over his pince-nez, benignly tweak eager consciences with conundrums about minor breaches of social etiquette like, say, pushing old tractors over cliffs and claiming for new ones on insurance, and, with a final flourish of his flowing white locks and elegantly embossed pocket watch, let them depart in peace. After all, the new for old tractor routine was about as serious as not plumping up the cushions on the sofa. And, in the farming community, about as common.

Which was all the more reason to lament being forced to watch so many devout parishioners depart, peacefully or otherwise, not merely god's house but this world as well. So not part of the plan.

And watching those Sunday circuit survivors whose rubric rebelled against doing anything peacefully was a particularly painful duty. Ministering to that caucus in the congregation. That not so covert coven. For whom hating their fellow woman seemed the primary article of faith. Odd that, among people of their persuasion. But then, Christianity is a broad church.

Mercifully, their machinations were no more visible to the other dear ladies than the Holy Ghost. So devout in their dotage. In their neatly coordinated couture, all delicate little frills and brooches, even sporting a spot of fur here and there. All soooo Celia.

The male members of the god-fearing gerontocracy were similarly sheltered. Gaily adorned as they were with paisley cravats and silky hankies, hanging out of the top pockets of their wide lapelled, tightly checked sports jackets. Neatly replete with leather elbow patches. The tiepins were a nice touch too. Terrifically Trevor.

Forget brief candles symbolising the brief span of our brief lives. This assembly was altogether *Brief Encounter*. They'd have found the plot a bit racy. But Noel would have found them simply too divine. Dears.

The value of divinity did, however, remain relative as far as The Coven was concerned. Its membership numbered three. And of its priorities, mutual hatred was number one.

Councillor Olive St Olave Tightarzz, mayor of the little town, was an absolute mare, indeed the mare from hell, as far as her sister Edith Egeria Ethcuse-me (née Tightarzz) was concerned.

Both were mere striplings relative to nearly all their co-religionists. Both dressed accordingly. Doffing their sartorial caps at at least the latter half of the last century. And both could be kindly. Sometimes. Though, to one another, never.

Neither could be quite sure now how the row had got so quite out of hand. Both had at times tried to extend the hand of friendship. But never had both been in the same mood at the same time. And timing IS everything. As any good comedian will tell you. Though it helps if you're in the room when he does so. Obviously.

But regardless of the rift's genesis, the apocalypse was nowhere. And Edith Egeria nursed her enduring loathing with all the sanctimonious passion she bestowed on Her Creator. On Sundays.

"Malevolent, malodorous mountain," was her description of choice for Olive. She avoided wherever possible words like "nasty" on account of her lisp. Likewise "excuse me". Which, annoyingly, she had to say rather often on account of her indisposition. Like the Reverend Buhmboil, it involved the backside. Only in her case it was a problem heard, not seen. Which could be a bit cheeky.

But there was symmetry in the spheres. Or at least between these two generously cut cuties. In that their invective was invariably evocative. Of bodily form. And functions.

"Flatulent fat moo," Olive called her sister. She didn't mince her words, or anything else. Indeed, parading round the parish, she looked like some sort of mythical monster. HALF human, but held up by tree-trunks.

Being mayor suited her nicely. She owned houses and land. And there were so many ways in which, in so selflessly serving the community, she could also serve herself handy little titbits. Here and there. OK, God works in mysterious ways, but god knows HOW they get away with it, sometimes, in town halls.

Still, she genuinely was diligent in her duties. Going to some lengths on some occasions to assist some of her lesser-heeled voters. Or siding with the unempowered against the over empowered. Her own colleagues, in short. Sometimes even in her own party.

Nonetheless, democracy, like divinity, remained a relative concept. Backscratching begetting baksheesh? What's a few bob between friends?

Edith Egeria had her down as the ugly face of capitalism. Though how she had the brass neck to think it is hard to imagine, seeing as she owned several shops in the town, and had signs up in all of them saying "Please do not ask for credit, as refusal often offends."

You don't often see that nowadays. Especially in a charity shop.

Of course, she'd leased out that premises at a massive discount. Which was massively decent of her. Though, admittedly, it was at the wrong end of the wrong street. And better, surely, to throw in a bit of goodwill than the towel.

No getting around it, or her for that matter, Edith Egeria was more preoccupied with prices than values. Fair, in her dealings, and honest, but a parable of the talents kind of girl. Which was why she always felt slightly uncomfortable when Reverend Buhmboil said things like: "Charity suffereth long, and is kind; charity is not puffed up."

His way of puffing up his all but concave chest while making such pronouncements struck her as particularly silly. "Eat your heart out, Arnold," she'd murmur darkly to herself. "Schwarzenegger you ain't."

But she wouldn't have missed chapel for the world. How could she, when it was her weekly joy, religious duty even, to view from her pew that She-Devil, that object of all her

Desire to Do Ill, that Beelzebub in a bonnet, that Olive St Olave Tightarzz.

"Faith, hope and love, and the greatest of these is love . . ." the Reverend Buhmboil would intone, while inwardly intimating to the Almighty that he would never learn to love his bottom. Faith lent him hope for miracles. But, alas, God would soon set him straight. As soon as he sat down.

As indifferent to the poor man's inner tribulations as to his outward injunctions, Councillor Olive St Olave Tightarzz enjoyed his performances. As the longer he went on the longer she could spend strangling her sister in that look of pure, satisfying, unadulterated malice. Matched only by the laser beam of white hot hatred she got in return. Forget Cain and Abel, these guys made marauding Viking slash'n'burn boys seem like a Friendly Society.

And yet Olive's hatred was mingled with fear. Fear that her own grotesquely guilty secret might one day be exposed. She was TICKLISH. Ridiculously, almost incontinently so. And this was her problem. Do it to her and she was no better than her sister at keeping all quiet on the postern front.

A bit like Noddy in his dear little car going "parp, parp". Amplified. Till it was more what you'd get from a multiple pile-up in Toytown. Or the resurrection of Jesus. The Last Trumpet.

So how could That Beast, that bucket of sick on legs, have been so vile, so long ago, to have pronounced, in the

121

f

hearing, what's more, of Great Auntie Flo, that death-sentence sentence: "Tickle Tightarzz with a feather."

Dear Great Auntie Flo, that third member of the Chapel Coven club, beetling away for so long, now finally ebbing away. Over the soggy mudflats of history. Hovering at the Gates of Heaven. To be received into the Bosom of Abraham. A long awaited reward for all those prayers spoken at chapel. Week after week. Decade after decade, for God's sake.

She'd been born a meek little thing. Inheriting the earth Reverend Buhmboil would have so loved to have glimpsed. Where kids effortlessly elided from Sunday school to chapel to pillarhood of the community.

But as the years rolled by the frontiers of religion-driven hegemony rolled back. And the ship of state in which she'd planned a pivotal post on the bridge now seemed landlocked. On an altogether different, altogether indifferent, terrain.

It turned her soul, once almost saintly, sour. Deprived of her world, she derived her joy from the discomfort of strangers. And nearest and dearest. Bitter truth being, that was the best bit.

Even now, as the valley of the shadow of death drew close, her mind burned bright. And as the family gathered round her bed, with the Reverend Buhmboil acting as a sort of United Nations peacekeeping force, she decided to atone for at least one sin. She'd loved committing it at the time. But she wasn't going to get any more out of it now.

She had indeed been privy, sitting in the privy, to the ruck that had ruptured relations between her great-nieces. When dear, sweet, spotty little Olive thought she heard Edith utter those dreaded words about tickling Tightarzz with a feather.

Oh, the outpourings! Like two she-cats, caterwauling and wailing. Biting, spitting, scratching, excoriating and extracting hair. So much of it. In clumps. From both the dear little darlings. Thus sealing a pact of mutual loathing never to be broken. As they thought.

By then, Great Auntie Flo, trading as a sweet, frail, god-fearing, loveable old lady, was strutting in borrowed plumes. Being as she now was a right bitch. An embittered old crone. Which was why she so swiftly pulled her knickers up, pulled the girlies apart and only pretended to try and soothe their stricken hearts.

She deliberately did not correct the misunderstanding that had caused the conflagration. How could she, when there was so much sport to be had, watching the fun? A blood feud? Between those two? Did her old heart good!

But now, finally, on her deathbed, on the breaking of wind, she broke silence.

"You remember, dears," she quavered, fixing the sisters with her still-steely gaze, "that day you fell out when you were scarce fallen from the chrysalis of the cradle."

Oh yes, they remembered.

"Well, my dear innocent little babes," she almost inaudibly intoned, thus forcing the siblings closer to her, and excruciatingly close to one another (amazing how annoying and selfish old people can be when they're about to die): "I think there may have been a tiny misapprehension when Edith seemed to say: Tickle Tightarzz with a feather.

"Her words that miserable, dank day have come back to me," she murmured. Softly, expiringly, but exploding with inward mirth. "She said . . . particularly nasty weather."

And so Great Auntie Flo fluttered off. To her own tormented Valhalla. Happy in her bequest to her great nieces. The knowledge that they'd spent almost their entire lives making complete idiots of themselves.

But the bequest begat good. Since The Row really had been about nothing, there was only one thing for it. The sisters made up. Thirty years down the line. Three hundred and sixty months. One thousand, five hundred and sixty weeks. Ten thousand, nine hundred and fifty-seven days. Nearly two hundred and sixty-three thousand hours. Almost sixteen million minutes. Over nine hundred and forty-six million seconds.

Still, better late than never.

After nurturing their nastiness for so long, they felt odd laying to rest this comfortingly redeeming vice. A bit like when the hiccups stop after hours and hours. Or taking off painful and clumsy calipers on discovering, after half a lifetime, that the polio was actually a misdiagnosed bruise.

No doubt about it, hatred is a heavy burden. In one of his more risqué sermons, Reverend Buhmboil had preached on the subject, with one eye on The Coven, and the other, doubtless with the aid of a mirror, on that which remained at the rear of his affections. His bottom.

"Oh God have mercy on the sinners," he'd exhorted. "Even for Austrian Adolf. Weigh the weight of hatred bearing down on his soul, for all those millions of Jews, Gypsies, homosexuals, and cripples. All of the time."

His theme was that the rage rampaging through the man's heart must have been well nigh unbearable. Had he been resurrected, he pondered, would he really want to do it all over again? Stand once more for the German parliament? On a third time lucky ticket?

In deference to his congregation's stylistic sensibilities, he forbore reference to his hope that nowadays that ridiculous coiffure and moustache would be enough on their own to bar the old monster from office. Reverend Buhmboil was a merciful man.

And, in ensuing years, God too blessed him with his kindly side. With the now reconciled sisters he formed a limited liability company, part funded with lottery money, to do much needed good works for needy good folk. Some of them even started showing up at chapel. A neat little spinoff.

Councillor Olive St Olave Tightarzz, with all her connections and contrivances, proved a dab hand at raising the cash. And Edith Egeria Ethcuse-me was financially formidable, even getting a special deal on the specially converted conveyance needed to cart the old dears around.

The best of it, from the dog-collared driver's point of view, was the driver's seat. Constructed as it was on the lines of a voluminous potty, the Reverend Buhmboil was potty about it. Understandable, from his underside's point of view.

And, as relations thawed between the erstwhile enemies, they blossomed between the Reverend and the Mayor. Blissfully. Bizarrely even, given their previous predisposition to preserve privacy. At all costs.

At all events, they got it together. And got married. At being made chief bridesmaid, Edith Egeria was tickled pink. But the Lord delivered her from temptation. Though the siblings were now on touchingly touching terms, there were still areas of sensitivity best avoided.

And so it came to pass that the Reverend Gargoyle relinquished the role, common to all unconjoined clergymen, of permanent public temptation. While Olive St Olave traded the title Tightarzz for Buhmboil.

Once more, symmetry in the spheres! Once more, raise your glasses to your maker! Bottoms up!

8

Calling the Shots

Ebenezer Pengeyser was venerated in the village. To adults, an object of awe. To kids, more just an object. As, they reasoned, no one can be well over a hundred, still staggering around, still compos mentis and not on the compost heap. It can't be done.

You could sort of see their point. Looking at this creaking, croaking, crop-haired old cadaver. Beret and brass badge on top. Definitely more parade ground than Prada.

But he still wobbled around on his ancient Western Flyer. And never trusted the new breed of four wheeler peelers. Though he did admit that Land's End to Launceston would be a bit of a trek. On a bike.

So how DID he do it? Give up the gaspers, like me, he always said. A good tip. Though not very helpful to very many people. Seeing as he was ninety-five at the time.

The name Ebenezer, meaning "stone of help, foundation

stone", suited him. He HAD been around as long as half the houses in the hamlet, and he could be very helpful, when he chose.

And when he chose not, he could make Genghis Khan seem a thoroughly reasonable person. This has to be an old person's perk, putting two fingers up to anyone, anywhere, on any grounds you think fit. The trick is, not being dead.

Ebenezer had outlived them all. Sometimes he felt he too had died, and come back as a ghost. Old Hamlet, stalking the battlements. Remember me. Remember me?

He remembered so many so long gone. Their quirky charms. Annoying habits. Little ways. Way of Life. Now, all up with the angels. Or up the swanee. Depending on your point of view.

As a kid, though as in a dream, he recalled his known world ending where his legs gave out. Shanks' mare was the nearest folk like him got to horsepower. Which was not even close.

Close communities, then. The villagers making their own amusement. And war on anyone from anywhere else. They'd dance on the streets, on high days and holidays. On god knows what locally brewed hooch. To the tune of god knows what pagan powers, half the time.

Still, the living for the Rector was easy. Unlike for the likes of Ebenezer. While the squire's idea of hard times was the third Sunday in the month. When the second under-butler had his afternoon off. Outrageous.

The great change came with the Great War. For Ebenezer, and for everyone else. To this day, when touching people up for free drinks, he'd say "vin blanc" or "vin rouge, s'il vous plait". This was no guarantee of a place in the Sorbonne, but a start.

In 1918 he'd joined up, just as the game was up, for the Hun. Though he made it to Cambrai. And that made him special. Cambrai being so much further than Camborne. It could as easily have been Camelot for all anyone he knew knew.

And he was one lucky Tommy. Because he didn't just go, he came back. Lungs, legs, and wits intact. And his bits. Which he treasured. As chaps do.

Tanks had made all the difference. Horses had turned out to be really rubbish at running into machine gun fire and staying alive at the same time. But these converted tractors were really much more sturdy.

Besides, the boffins' policy of chucking failed prototypes of these new top secret weapons down mineshafts, so the Hun wouldn't get his hands on the technology, gave the farmers an idea. That discarded tractors could be more use dead than alive.

Private Pengeyser learned lots from his one and only foray into France, and out of Cornwall. Like not doffing his cap at carriage customers who were actually idiots. And not hating Teddy Treweddy for wedding a lass from another village. Just two miles away? Too far by miles, the word was.

Edwardian Cornishmen did have a long way to go. But they did know how to look after themselves. And not look to outsiders to do it for them. What with their productive industries like farming, fishing and mining. And service industries, like smuggling, wrecking and poaching.

And, post-Versailles, add to that list that tip they picked up during the hostilities and adapted for peacetime use. Turning swords into ploughshares, sort of. In this case, pushing old tractors down cliff sides and claiming for new ones on insurance. So much more cost effective than clambering up cliff sides and trying to quarry them. And so much more fun too.

Just like the movies. Ebenezer loved Charlie Chaplin. And heartily agreed with him that no one wanted to hear actors talking. Likewise that a day without laughter is a wasted day.

Admittedly, there was that lost decade, after he was first widowed, when he went quiet. Till he met Missus number two and perked up again. Explaining he wasn't really eccentric. But had just been in a very bad mood. For ten years.

And after Noonoo, then Nada, came Nell. Twenty-five happy years with each. A marvellous party. It was hell when they died, of course. But he'd been through that before. In France. And was still grateful about those bits. Of his.

Thanks to them, there were the kids. Who were such a comfort. Followed by grandkids. And great grandkids. And great great grandkids. And, great Scott, great great great grandkids too.

It's said that cuddly Khan fellow has sixteen million descendants now living. Which, by anyone's reckoning, is a hard act to follow. But Ebenezer had given it a go.

And all those Pengeysers popping out everywhere presented a reassuringly familiar picture when the unknown world called on Cornwall once a year. Called it such a lovely place. And called the shots.

Call the old fellow old-fashioned, but sometimes it made him spit. Actually, he never could quite get used to the new-fangled absence of signs prohibiting spitting in pubs. But when he gave up the gaspers he kicked that habit too. Mostly.

His kicking days were now over, however. However much he felt like it sometimes. He'd heard in the pub one night about some old Greek bloke, who'd be off to an uninhabited island each summer because he couldn't stand all those tourists, who made his world unrecognisable.

Ebenezer didn't know where old Papa-dapala-who'dyoumer-thingy came from. But he did know where he was COMING from. From a place of pride and self-respect, as he saw it.

Was he deluding himself? Did he care, even if he was? Of course not. Though he did care, now and then, to delude others, visitors, in the name of sweet revenge.

That dish, best served cold, could be just as tasty on hot

summer's days. And Ebenezer savoured it, when it fell, as perchance it might, neatly on to his plate. Like his worst enemies' kidneys, devilled. Delicious.

"I say old chap," some chap called out haughtily, as one bequeathing a special kindness on some distant poor relation in the great family of humanity. "Would you kindly . . ."

"A little more than kin and less than kind," or words to that effect, Ebenezer growled to himself. He was feeling especially grumpy that day on account of his gout. Which he didn't deserve, seeing as he wasn't a drink-sodden fat slob. Couldn't afford to be, more's the pity.

"Of course, sirrrrrr. Anything to oblige, sirrrrrr," he said, bowing deeply in mock Respect for his Betters. Guys like that really got his goat. At such times he would smile and smile and be a villain while he smiled. Or at least be as vile as he could without getting hacked to pieces in return.

"Very, very kind," murmured the person. "I wonder, could you tell me how long's the cliff walk from here to the next cove. Doesn't look far on my map."

It didn't. Because it wasn't. But the map omitted the salient detail that the path was a succession of salients. Up hill and down dale. Seriously steep climbing. All the way. If you had the tiniest bit of a dodgy ticker, or were more hip replacement than hip, you were doomed. Either way, it was going to take hours. Or the rest of your life, depending on the pacemaker.

"Arrrrrrrrr, ten minutes," said Ebenezer. Gleefully. Knowing the gullible idiot, this awful orficer type, would believe him. And, even if his days were not well and truly ended, this one would be well and truly spoiled.

"Charming, charming. You local chaps, especially chaps like you, always such a fount of wisdom," pattered the patronising git. Adding: "A bit more respect for age wouldn't go amiss anywhere. I can tell you must be pushing eighty if a day."

At this Ebenezer momentarily stopped in his tracks. Not that he was going anywhere fast. You don't, when you're past a hundred. But he did wonder, just for a moment, whether he might have been a bit hasty. In his rush to judgement.

But, hell, he'd said it now. Ten minutes. Dreckly. Cornish time's different from everyone else's. Everyone knows that. At least, everyone in Cornwall.

No surprise then, that the soon to be footsore fellow from upcountry didn't. And did feel pretty sore at being had. When he had, after all, meant no disrespect to the old chap.

And yet. And yet. . . Maybe his manner might have sounded a bit offhand. Maybe he should have engaged the good man in a few preliminary pleasantries. Asked him about the bearbaiting, or the sheep worrying, or the ritual sacrifice of infants, or whatever it was the natives liked to get up to in these parts.

Poor Captain Fitz-Ferdinand. During his good spell in the

army he'd had a good time. Travelled the world. Met interesting people. And killed them. Such a lark. Ask General Genghis.

But fraternising with the fellows, the other ranks, was not encouraged in his day. Practically a hanging offence. So he'd never quite got the hang of it.

Demobilised, he got dispirited. Not that he missed murdering people exactly. It was more the camaraderie. Even the barrack room banter from which he'd been almost exclusively excluded.

But, like Ebenezer when the Nada nuptials beckoned, he cheered up. When he worked out a way of getting together with the chaps again. Getting together a charity, minting medals for men who made it past Dunkirk, past D-Day, past VE day, and still hadn't passed on.

Right now though, he felt he'd better get a move on. After that last hateful hill and that last big push that nearly had him pushing up the daisies. Besides, sprightly though HE was, old codgers who'd coshed the Boche were falling like flies these days. Frightening.

Still, half a gallon of good old Cornish mead in the good old Cornishmen's Arms quelled the coward in him. And got him happily humming Noel's nice little ditty: "Don't let's be beastly to the Germans."

He'd just got to the bit about them giving us culture, art and music to excess, as well as two world wars and Rudolf Hess, when something made him start. And stop.

It was a distinctly familiar voice, saying in a distinctly Cornish accent, "Vin rouge, s'il vous plait."

He listened incredulously, if slightly hazily, to the teetering tones of the centenarian seer. And homespun homilies about giving up smoking when you're ninety-five, and watching out for horseless carriages as the gentry drive terribly when tiddly. Which is anytime after breakfast time. Sometimes even earlier.

"They'm 'ad to learrrrn a thing or two on they there French roads, though, they there officers in my lot in the Duke o' Cornwall's Light Infantry," the old fellow went on, confidentially. "Second battalion we was. Kicked the Kaiser right up the kharzi."

At this, Captain Archie Fitz-Ferdinand choked on his mead, nearly, and leapt to his feet, nearly. And fell flat on his face, nearly. This old monster's mob disbanded in 1918.

His discreetly waxed moustache twitched. His sandy, Sandhurst-styled hair stood on end. His tropically blotchy complexion, born in Borneo and Korea, turned a whiter shade of pale. Well beyond the pale. As all previous conquests paled into insignificance.

Another song suggested itself. "Happy Christmas from Korea, land of lice and diarrhoea." Christmases? All his had come at once.

He felt like he'd gone fly fishing, and landed a whale. Or ordered a steak and got the herd. Or, having picked up a

Picasso for pennies at a car boot, found it was an original. Strike a light, this was striking gold.

After all, these chaps were no more supposed to be living among us than the Angel of Mons. A doubtful proposition even back in the trenches.

Though Ebenezer too sometimes had his doubts about things, looking round the pub. It was still where it had always been. But what was all that there carpet trade? Where was the sawdust? And what was that there noisy contraption people put coins in? When all it did was flash lights at you, like so many whizz-bangs.

Still, he liked the fact everyone took his advice and didn't smoke any more. At least not in the bar. One mission accomplished at least.

And the Captain was on another. To be accomplished at all costs. He'd played the detective all these years. And he really was going to get his man. Next to all those minor burglars of World War Two, Ebenezer Pengeyser was a Great Train Robber.

"I say old chap," he blurted out, immediately experiencing an uncomfortable sensation that he'd used those words before and it had ended badly. "I say, my DEAR old chap," he corrected himself, "my DEAR old chap, would you mind frightfully joining me, if I joined you, in a stoop or two of vin rouge. Or vin blanc. Or whatever jolly old colour you care to name.

"You see, I'm campaigning for special medals for special

chaps who did the bish bash Boche thing, don't you know.

"Of course, an exception must be made for chaps like you. Due to an act of gross insubordination that has come to my attention in the last twenty-four hours, you're to be made an example of. You are to appear before a court martial. And be shot at dawn".

But, as he said this, was there a hint of a glint in his eye? A glint of mirth? Oh yes. He couldn't help it. And Ebenezer couldn't help but notice it.

He was canny like that. They officers were a queer breed. But he'd got over the idea that if it moves, salute it, and if it doesn't, whitewash it. He'd learned instead to look at it. And listen. And learn.

And here, in spite of everything, or in Frog-lingo *malgré tout*, this being one other bit of French he'd picked up at The Front, *malgré tout* here was the beginning of a beautiful, if of necessity rather short-lived, friendship. Between ex cavalry officer of modern times, and ex poor bloody infantryman of so long ago.

Of course, the song helped. Ebenezer had told his little stories about the fighting and the fags so many times that he scarcely heard himself speak. Which left him free to listen to others instead.

The notion of not being beastly to the Germans had struck him at first as totally yellow-bellied. Anyway, that Coward cove was simply too avant garde for a man of his upbringing. Too clever by half. Too many words. Too many notes, for god's sake.

But Ebenezer liked to think he moved with the times. A thoroughly modern man. Besides, maybe Noel was not the nitwit he'd had him down as after all. Given that the War to End All Wars hadn't quite done what it said on the tin.

So he'd warmed to the warbler at the next table, even before he told him about the medal. And bought him all that vin rouge, mercy buckets.

He said sorry for his little joke about the jaunt, and got his gong. Or at least the promise of it. As the two men made up and made music together. Singing the world to rights as only military men know how.

It was a full house that night at the Cornishmen's, the crowd swelled by a visiting coach party of Czech, Polish and Dutch tourists.

Perhaps they were expecting a bit of local colour in this cosy little local. A bit of Cornish crooning in this cocooned little world. But a couple of sloshed old soldiers serenading them about Hitler must surely have seemed a bit much.

Especially the words justifying the German war effort on the grounds: "Though they've been a little naughty to the Czechs and Poles and Dutch, I can't believe those countries . . . really minded very much."